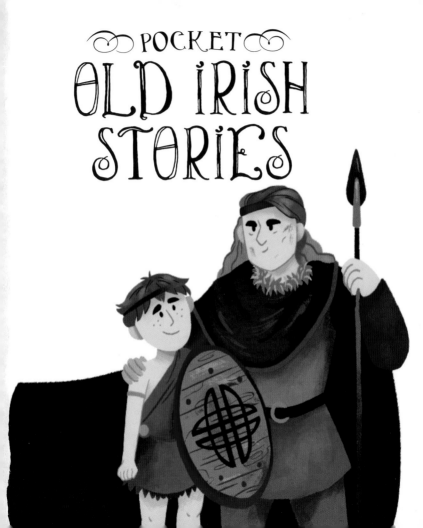

POCKET
OLD IRISH STORIES

Gill Books
Hume Avenue, Park West, Dublin 12

www.gillbooks.ie

Gill Books is an imprint of M.H. Gill & Co.

Copyright © Teapot Press Ltd 2019

ISBN: 978-0-7171-7942-8

This book was created and produced by Teapot Press Ltd

Retold by Fiona Biggs
Illustrated by Marina Pessarrodona
Designed by Tony Potter

Printed in Europe

This book is typeset in Sabon Infant

A CIP catalogue record for this book is available
from the British Library.

5 4 3 2 1

POCKET
OLD IRISH STORIES

Stories retold by Fiona Biggs
Illustrated by Marina Pessarrodona

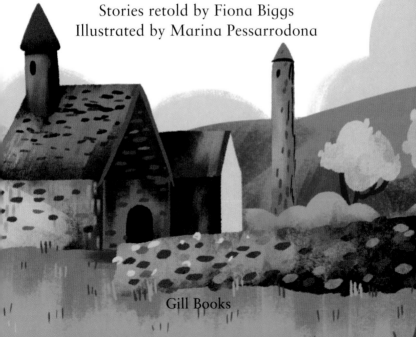

Gill Books

Contents

The Luck of the O'Donoghue

In the years that followed the Great Hunger in Ireland the people once again had enough to eat, but their lives were difficult. They worked hard so that they could eat, and they ate so that they would be strong enough to work.

Every evening, after a long day working in the fields, a widow woman, Mrs O'Brien, her son Seán and his wife Kitty sat around the fire in their one-room cottage after a simple meal of potatoes and milk. They couldn't afford to buy candles, so the only light in the room came from the turf burning in the hearth. They passed the time by telling tales of long ago, when life in Ireland was good and all the people had enough

food to eat and were happy and free to live their lives the way they wanted to.

One evening, as the little family huddled close to the fire for warmth, Mrs O'Brien told them the story of The O'Donoghue, a king who had reigned hundreds of years ago.

'The O'Donoghue was a fierce warrior and a wise and just king. He was fair to everyone, rich and poor, and he even punished his own son when he broke one of his laws. People said that he was so wise he had been given the gift of prophecy. It was known that anyone who got close to him had great luck in life.

'The king loved to see all his friends and he hosted huge feasts with lots of food and mead. People came from far and wide to enjoy his hospitality and to hear his wise words. In the custom of the time, the bards

who travelled the length and breadth of Ireland came
to the feasts to entertain the guests in exchange for
food and drink and a place to sleep. They sang songs
about the heroes of the olden days and their noble
deeds, and about the wise king who was their host.

'One night, when the bard had finished singing and
had joined the company at the table, the king himself
began to speak of the times that would come in Ireland.
He said that the good and noble men of Ireland would
fight and die for their country, and that they would

be betrayed. There would be bravery and cowardice, and there would be glory and shame. There would be wealth and honour, but there would also be great sorrow throughout the land.

'The guests at the feast were filled with wonder and pride, but they also shivered with fear, for the king had spoken of evil things to come. What would become of their children in those dark times?

'As they thought about what the king had said, he got up from his place at the head of the banqueting table, walked across the great hall, went through the heavy oak doors that led outside and walked down to the lake. The guests followed him out of the great hall. Instead of stopping at the water's edge, the king walked across the lake, as if the water were solid. The moon was shining on the lake and everyone could see the king as he walked farther and farther out towards

the middle of the lake. He turned, raised his arm in a salute to his people and then he was gone.

'And although the people waited and waited by the lakeside, they never saw the king again, not as long as they lived. They waited and hoped for his return, for he was a good king and they felt the need of him in the days that followed.'

Mrs O'Brien gazed into the fire, a faraway look on her face.

'No,' she said. 'They never saw their king again. But after they were all dead, others saw him. And I have seen him,' she added.

Seán and Kitty looked at her in amazement. They thought she must have gone mad.

'Each year, on the first day of May, the king can be seen at sunrise, riding across the lake on a beautiful white horse. Not everyone can see him, but if you do, you'll have good luck as you go through life.'

'And when did you see him?' asked Seán.

'Well,' said Mrs O'Brien, 'as you know, my family lived here, beside the Lakes of Killarney, when I was a girl. At dawn on the first day of May one year I was standing in the doorway of our cottage watching the sunrise. I looked across to the lake and, although the day was calm, there were white horses on the water. Suddenly a big wave appeared out of nowhere and moved towards me. I was afraid and I shrank back, even though I knew the wave couldn't reach me. And it was then that I saw the king, riding on the crest of the great wave.

'He was sitting on his great white horse, his silver armour gleaming in the sun and his dark hair

streaming behind him. He was preceded by the most beautiful beings I have ever seen, dressed in flowing garments in all the colours of the rainbow. They carried baskets of pearls and they kept putting their hands into the baskets and scattering handfuls of pearls as they moved through the water so that the air itself was shimmering. They had garlands of flowers over their arms and they threw the flowers up into the air so that they landed in front of the king. The air was full of sweet perfume and music that seemed to come from heaven.

'As I watched, the king and his entourage came closer and closer, so that I thought they would soon be close enough for me to touch them. But then they seemed to melt away into the landscape. I breathed in the last of the perfumed air and went back inside.'

'And that was that?' asked Kitty.

'Well, I knew that whoever saw the O'Donoghue and was close enough to smell the perfume that seemed to surround him would get some of the good luck that he always left behind him. He certainly left some of that luck with me. That summer some young Dublin ladies came to stay in Killarney, and when they heard that I had seen the king they came to visit me and asked me about my vision. After I had told them my story they asked my father if I could go back with them to Dublin to train as a lady's maid. He didn't

want me to leave but he knew that it would be a good opportunity for me, better than any he could provide, and he would have a bit more for the other children, who were all younger than me. So off I went to Dublin and a much better life. The ladies were very kind to me, paid me well and gave me good training. They taught me how to read and write and even took me to London a few times – and if you think Dublin is grand, you should see that city. You couldn't imagine the riches to be found there!

'And then I met your father, Seán, and that was another bit of good luck for me. He worked for my ladies as a coachman. We saved all our wages, got married and took a little farm back here in Killarney. We were lucky to have a good landlord, but when the potato crop failed and failed again there were bad times for everybody – potatoes rotted in the ground and people were dying of hunger, cold and fever. Those were dark, dark days, but we lived through them, so perhaps that was the O'Donoghue luck again. So many of our friends and neighbours didn't survive and most of those who did went to America.

'Then you were born, but by then our landlord had lost all his money and we had moved to another farm, with a bad landlord. Your father lost all hope and died of the disappointment about the way our lives had turned out. I thought then that the O'Donoghue

luck had been used up. And maybe it had, but it had brought us many good times and I'm grateful for that.

'One thing I know for sure is that there's plenty of that O'Donoghue luck out there and a few lucky people will get some of it if they happen to see the king riding the crest of the wave. If you take yourselves down to the lakeside at dawn next May Day you might catch a glimpse of him and smell the perfume that will bring good fortune into your lives.'

The Young Piper

Some time ago in Tipperary there was a hardworking couple who lived on the estate of the big house in that area. The husband, Joseph, worked on the farm for the landlord, and the mother, Brigid, ran the home and looked after the children. They had five beautiful sons, sturdy and golden-haired, who never gave their parents a moment's worry.

Joseph and Brigid were the envy of all their neighbours, but no one begrudged them their good fortune because they were a kind and generous couple, always willing to help out those in need.

After some years the couple had a sixth child, yet another son, but this one was sickly and crotchety and for a long time it was thought that he wouldn't live past his first birthday. He looked completely different from his healthy golden-haired brothers – his hair was jet black and matted, his teeth were crooked and yellow and his limbs were thin. No matter how much he ate he never seemed to grow. He was always whining and crying, and the only member of the family who had any patience with him at all was his mother, Brigid, who loved him dearly.

Whenever the neighbours came to visit they had lots of advice for Brigid.

'There's something not right with that child,' they'd say. 'Are you sure it's not a changeling?'

But if Brigid had any thoughts like that she kept them to herself, and soon the neighbours just accepted the strange child who was always hovering in the background, grunting instead of talking, greedily eating the cakes his mother put out for the visitors. In fact, he seemed to eat more than his five older brothers put together, although you'd never have known it to look at him.

Things went on like that for a while until, one day, when the child was about five years old, the blind piper was doing his rounds of the area and he called on the household. He sat down beside the fire and he had his bellow under his arm and the pipe in his mouth as soon as he'd wet his whistle with a cup of tea.

He had no sooner begun to play a rousing tune than the child, who had been asleep in his little bed on the other side of the fire, woke up and began to kick his legs and wave his arms in time to the music. He reached out for the pipes and Brigid asked the piper if he could borrow them.

'You'll have to tell me how to strap them on,' she said, but as soon as the child had hold of the pipes he had himself fitted into the straps and was piping away as if his life depended on it.

And it was no raucous caterwauling that he produced out of the pipes. It was as if he'd had 20 years' practice at them. The blind piper, of course, didn't realise that the musician was hardly five years old, and it wasn't until the astonished neighbours came crowding into the house that someone told him.

'He must be a natural genius,' he said. 'I've been playing for 30 years and I've never been as good as that!'

The boy played jigs and reels and ballads and he soon had everyone dancing.

The piper offered to take him on as an apprentice, but Brigid couldn't bear the thought of parting with her youngest son. When the time came for the piper to leave, she had to pull the pipes out of the boy's clutches, and he screamed and shouted until his father came home that evening.

Brigid told Joseph what had happened, and they decided that if the boy had his own pipes he'd always be able to make a living for himself. But pipes were not cheap, and the next fair day Joseph drove his prize pig to market and used the money he got for her to order a child-sized set of pipes.

Well, about two weeks later the pipes arrived, and there had never been so much excitement in the household. The boy strapped himself into them and immediately started playing jigs and reels.

After that, the house was never without the sound of music coming from it, flowing out of the windows and doors and up through the chimney. The young piper's fame spread far and wide and it was soon said that there wasn't a piper in the whole county of Tipperary that was even half as good.

The young girls and lads began to come to the family's house in the evenings, for there wasn't better dancing to be had in the 10 parishes around. Whatever tunes the little piper played seemed to put wings under the girls' feet, and the boys' steps were as quick as lightning. On and on they twirled and tapped, and many a match was made after an evening of dancing in Joseph and Brigid's kitchen.

After a few months the dancers began to notice that they were having a hard time keeping up with the music. Their feet became tangled up and they were forever falling over and landing on their backs on the kitchen floor. The girls and lads stopped coming to the house, but the piper kept on piping.

He piped the cups off their hooks and the plates off the dresser, and soon the pots and pans were flying around the kitchen. The stools and chairs moved around the room as if they were bewitched, and before long everyone in the family had tripped over one at least once. The family's cat and dog, who had a long habit of sleeping in front of the fire, refused to come inside the house any more, and slept outdoors in all weathers.

Soon the neighbours stopped calling in, for they were likely to land on the floor when the chair they

sat on was piped out from under them. And then the mischief seemed to spread further afield. The sheep on the hills got the staggers and died and the cows in the milking shed began to kick over the full buckets of milk. Barns began to collapse for no reason at all and the crops in the fields died as soon as they started growing. It didn't take long for the neighbours to remember their old suspicions about the young piper and soon the blame for all of the misfortune in the county was laid at Brigid and Joseph's door.

One Sunday, Joseph's employer called in to see him after Mass.

'I'm afraid I'll have to let you go,' he said sadly. 'You're a good worker, but this lad of yours is having a terrible effect on the neighbourhood. I'll give you a good reference, but you're to be gone by the end of the week.'

This was terrible news, but Joseph had a decent reputation and he'd soon found a good job on a farm in the next county, where people hadn't heard about his musical son. The family packed up all their belongings in their cart, said goodbye to their neighbours and set off for their new home. The dog and cat refused to go, and parked themselves on the doorstep of a more peaceful neighbour, who took them in out of pity for the animals, and out of gratitude that the troublesome piper was going away.

Brigid and Joseph's new home was just half a day's journey away, but it seemed to be a very long journey indeed. They had hidden the pipes, so their youngest child was shouting and roaring from the top of the cart until they were all almost deafened. When everyone's nerves were completely frayed Brigid gave in and handed over the pipes, hoping for a few minutes' peace.

The child was just strapping them on when they came to a bridge over the river.

'I'm not crossing that!' he shouted. 'You've played a mean trick bringing me here!'

And he struggled and shouted and jumped out of the cart, with his pipes, and he jumped right into the river! The river was full and swirling, and there were currents and waves that would take a grown man under the water.

'Oh my poor boy, my poor boy!' wept Brigid. 'He'll drown!'

Her five older boys ran to the other side of the bridge and after a couple of seconds they saw their brother coming through, sitting on the surface of the swirling water, piping away merrily. He was soon whirled away, and although his brothers ran along the bank they soon lost sight of him when the water went round a bend.

The young piper was never seen again in those parts. His mother was the only one who mourned his loss, and even she eventually agreed that her musical son had probably been a changeling after all. The family prospered in their new situation and soon Joseph was able to buy a small farm. Although they enjoyed living in their peaceful home the whole family agreed that it was sometimes just a bit too quiet.

The Widow's Son

Once upon a time there was a widow who lived in a little cottage with her son Tom. Her husband had died a long time ago and Tom had looked after his mother for years. He was well known in the area as a kind and hard-working boy, who was as truthful as the day was long.

One autumn, after the second bad harvest in a row, Tom decided to leave home to find some work, so that his mother would at least not have the burden of feeding him. There was a bag of flour in the cupboard and an old hen in the farmyard, so Tom asked his mother to make a loaf of bread out the of flour and to roast the bird – he said he would take half of each and be on his way.

His mother did as he asked and came to the gate with him.

'Would you like half the loaf and half the chicken with my blessing, or the whole of both of them with my curse?' she asked.

'Why, mother, I would never want your curse. Give me the half of the loaf and the half of the chicken and I'll be on my way.'

But the old woman put the whole loaf and the whole bird into his satchel.

'A thousand blessings on you, son,' she said, as Tom set off down the road with tears in his eyes.

Tom walked all day, calling in at every farmhouse he passed to ask if there was any work going. But he was sent away each time, and soon he was tired and night was falling. Just as he was wondering where he could lay his head for the night he heard a donkey braying loudly. He followed the noise and came to the edge of a bog. There was a donkey stuck in the bog – he had sunk in up to his shoulders and hadn't a hope of getting out without help.

'Oh Tom,' called the donkey, 'please get me out of this bog before I drown!'

So Tom threw in as many stones and bits of wood as he could find and soon the donkey was able to find his feet and he scrambled out of the bog.

'Thank you, Tom,' he said. 'I'll do the same for you. Where are you off to this fine night?'

'I'm trying to find work,' said Tom. 'The harvest wa bad again.'

'I'll go with you, then,' said the donkey. 'Aren't two often better than one?'

When they came to the next village they were greete by a dog with a saucepan tied to his tail. He was being chased by a crowd of boys who were all throwing ston at him. The donkey let out the loudest bray you have ever heard and the boys turned and ran away.

Tom untied the saucepan from the dog's tail.

'Why don't you come with us?' he said. 'We'll keep you safe from horrible boys.'

So the trio walked on down the road until they cam to a small clearing by the side of the road behind a low wall. A path from the clearing led into the forest, which looked dark and uninviting.

'We can sleep here tonight,' said Tom. He sat against the wall with the dog and shared his bread and roast chicken with him while the donkey found some grass and herbs. A hungry cat came along, his ribs sticking out through his thin fur and Tom gave him some chicken bones. As he was eating, a fox jumped over the wall with a fine black rooster flapping in his mouth. The dog chased after the fox, who dropped the rooster, and the poor bird fluttered back with the dog to thank Tom, who invited him to join the little band. Then they all settled down to sleep.

A few hours later they were all fast asleep when they were rudely awoken by the rooster, crowing as if dawn had already arrived.

'What's up? What's up?' brayed the donkey, who had been having a lovely dream about a beautiful meadow full of juicy grass. 'I can't see the dawn light –

why are you crowing, you stupid bird?'

'There's light over there,' said the rooster. 'I can see it breaking through the trees.'

'I can see it too,' said Tom, 'but it's candlelight, not the dawn. It seems to be coming from a house in the forest – we might as well go over and ask for shelter for the rest of the night.'

So they all shook themselves awake and set off towards the light. Soon they had reached a hollow in the forest with a house in the middle of it. It was not only light that was coming from it, but drunken singing and loud laughter.

'I'll have a look inside before we knock on the door,' said Tom. 'We don't know if these people are friendly.'

He climbed up on the donkey's back so that he could look in one of the windows. He saw six large men inside, sitting at a table, pulling large joints of meat apart and washing the food down with beer and wine. The men were all armed with knives, swords and guns, and Tom could see gold and silver and jewels overflowing from some sturdy little chests in the corner of the room.

'That was a great haul of treasure we got from his lordship!' shouted one.

'And here's to the good health of the porter at his gate!' yelled another.

Tom whispered to his companions and they all started making as much noise as they could.

'Hold your fire!' shouted Tom. 'Don't shoot until I give the order.' And they all started making noise again while Tom smashed the biggest window in the room. The wind blew out the candles and the robbers rushed out of the house, tripping over each other in the darkness.

Tom and the donkey and the dog and the cat and the rooster all piled into the house, closed the shutters, lit the candles again and ate until they were completely stuffed. Then they blew out the candles and settled down to get some sleep.

Little did they know that they hadn't seen the last of the robbers, who were annoyed to be out in the cold night air without food or drink to comfort them. And then there was all that treasure they'd just gone to the trouble of stealing!

'I'm going back,' said their leader, 'to see if I can get my hands on the treasure.' And off he went into the darkness. When he got to the house, the only light was the fire, so he went towards it, thinking to light a candle from it. He kicked the cat as he passed him and the cat went at him with tooth and claw. He stepped back and stood on the dog's tail and dog jumped on him, bringing him down to the ground, and bit his face and his arms and legs. He rushed out of the house, chased by the rooster, who pecked and scratched his face, and then the donkey kicked him from the front door to the manure heap. The robber staggered out of the manure and limped away as fast as his battered legs could carry him.

Before the sun had risen the following morning Tom and his merry band had a good breakfast, then Tom lashed the two treasure chests to the donkey and off they went to the lord's mansion. Tom asked to see the lord, but the porter didn't want to let him in.

'Perhaps you'd like to tell him who let the robbers into his house last night?' said the rooster, who had travelled on the donkey's head.

'What does he mean, Seamas?' asked the lord, who had come into the hallway.

'Take no notice of him,' said the porter scornfully. 'I certainly didn't open the door to the six robbers.'

'Well, if you didn't, you wouldn't have known there were six of them,' said the lord angrily. 'Get out of my sight and don't darken my door again!' he shouted, as the porter made his escape down the drive.

'Here's your treasure, so no harm done,' said Tom, pointing to the two chests on the donkey's back.

The lord found positions in his household for the donkey, dog, cat and rooster, and he saw to it that Tom was dressed in the finest clothes before he sat down to the finest meal he had ever eaten. The lord made Tom his steward and gave him his own house in the grounds. Tom brought his mother to live with him and they never wanted for anything again.

The Well of Down Derry

Once upon a time there was a king of Connacht who had three sons. You might think that the sons would have been given fine royal names, but the king and his wife had very little imagination, so they named the boys One, Two and Three. One and Two were short and swarthy, but Three was tall and graceful with a head of shining golden hair. At about the time that all three of them reached manhood the king became very ill. His doctors were unable to find a cure, no matter what they tried. The king was starved and then he was put into icy baths; he was fed a diet that was nothing but fat; he was filled full of whiskey and made to sleep outside in the fresh air, but nothing worked. Finally, the king sent for his druid, who prodded and poked the patient, then scratched his own head and stroked his chin.

'I have no remedy for you, your Majesty,' said the druid. 'The only thing that will cure you is a drink of water from the well of Down Derry. One sip of that water and you will be completely restored.'

'Well, that's no problem,' said the king. 'I have three fine sons who would do anything to save their father. Where is the well of Down Derry? I will give them instructions to go there immediately.'

But the druid didn't know where the well was located, and even though he went into a trance for a day and a night he still couldn't discover what county it was in.

The king sent for his sons and he told them that he needed them to find the well of Down Derry and fill a flask of water for him there. One, Two and Three were eager to set out on the quest for the well and the king gave each of them a purse of gold to help them along their way.

49

The three princes left the palace and went off down the road together. When they came to a crossroads they decided to go in three different directions, so that they would have more chance of finding the well.

There was a fine inn at the crossroads and One and Two thought it would be a good idea to have a meal before they separated. Soon they had drunk so much ale that they had forgotten why they had come along the road, and they decided to stay in the inn for the night.

Three, meanwhile, had decided not to delay, but to get on with the search for the well. The road he took was long and he didn't find any landmarks that he recognised. Night was falling and he had nowhere to lay his head for the night, but the moon was full and soon it was lighting his path along the road, so he kept going, although he was slowing down with every step he took. When he was feeling so tired he thought he'd fall down on the spot, he saw a small cabin in a clearing a little distance from the road, with smoke curling out of the chimney. What a welcome sight that was! Three knocked on the door of the cabin and went in, calling out a greeting to whoever might be there.

But the cabin was empty, so Three sat down in front of the fire and fell asleep. He slept until late the next morning and woke to the sound of someone sweeping the floor. He opened his eyes and saw an old woman tidying the room and getting ready to make his breakfast.

'Good morning, your Highness,' she said, when she saw that her guest was awake. 'You'll need a good breakfast after the long journey you made yesterday.'

'But how do you know who I am?' asked Three, puzzled.

'I'm wiser than I look,' said the old woman. 'I know that you are the youngest son of our king, who lies gravely ill in the palace. You have set out to find the well of Down Derry so that its water will cure your father. Tonight you will sleep here again, and tomorrow you can continue your journey. If you travel westwards, you will find the well.'

The old woman opened a little door in the corner of the room and showed Three into a magnificent bedroom with an enormous soft bed in the middle of it. He threw himself onto the bed and was asleep within seconds.

The next day he got up early and was out on the road after a quick breakfast.

'Keep going west,' called the old woman, as he disappeared down the road.

Three followed the road until the sun was going down. He didn't think his luck would repeat itself, so he was looking around for a place to sleep under the trees by the side of the road when he saw a cabin, identical to the one from the previous two nights, and he thought he must have walked in a complete circle.

He opened the door and went in, but the woman inside was much older than the one he had left that morning.

'I'm glad you got here safely, your Highness,' said the old woman. 'My sister told me to expect you tonight.'

'Your sister!' exclaimed Three.

'Yes, it was my sister who provided your hospitality

these last two nights,' said the old woman. 'You are now a day closer to the well of Down Derry.'

Three sat down beside the fire and ate the excellent meal the old woman had prepared for him. Then he went to bed in a room that was even finer than the last one he had slept in.

The next morning, after a good breakfast, Three prepared to leave, but when he opened the front door of the cabin there were three roads before him, each leading in a different direction.

'Which road do I take?' he asked the old woman. 'I don't know which one leads to the well of Down Derry.'

The old woman went back inside the cabin and came out holding a large ball of red wool.

'Roll this along the path before you and follow where it leads,' she said. 'It will guide you on your way.'

So Three rolled the ball of wool in front of him as he walked along the road and at the end of the day it stopped at the door of a small cabin.

Three went inside, expecting to find yet another old woman, but this time he was greeted by an old man.

'Welcome, your Highness,' he smiled. 'My sisters told me to expect you this evening. You are now very close to the well of Down Derry but your task is becoming more difficult. I will come with you on the next part of your journey.'

They left the cabin and went down to the river bank. The river was deep but the old man guided Three over some stones that made a path over the fast-flowing water. When they reached the opposite side they rested for a while. The old man pointed further down the valley and Three saw a castle rising up out of the mist.

'We have reached the well of Down Derry,' said the old man. 'It is in the cellar of that castle. The queen has been enchanted and she and all of her courtiers and servants are in a deep sleep. No one will stop you as you make your way to the well.'

He handed Three two small glass phials. 'Fill these with water from the well,' he instructed, 'and then come straight back. Don't allow yourself to be distracted by anything.'

Three set off for the castle, and when he got there he went straight to the cellar, passing sleeping servants in every passage. The well was in the middle of the floor and Three filled the two phials with the clear water that bubbled up from it. On his way back from the cellar he took a shortcut through the queen's quarters, glancing into the banqueting hall, where the queen and all her courtiers sat around the table, fast asleep. The queen was so beautiful Three couldn't resist kissing her as he went past, then he hurried out of the castle and back to the river bank where the old man was waiting for him. They went back to the old man's cabin, where Three handed him the two phials of water.

'One is for your father,' said the old man. 'The other is for me and my sisters, who have been bewitched.' He drank some water from the phial and was transformed into a handsome prince right before Three's eyes.

'Think what the water will do for your father,' said the prince. 'Hurry home with it so that he can be made well again.'

Three left the prince, sprinting back along the road he had taken as fast as he possibly could. In less time than it had taken him to travel to the well, he was back at the junction where he had left his two brothers. One and Two were still in the inn, drinking their purses empty.

'I found the well!' shouted Three, waving the phial of water triumphantly.

'This calls for a celebration,' said One, and the two older brothers filled a glass for the youngest member of their family. They kept filling it until he was in a drunken stupor, then they took the phial and ran back to the palace.

The king was close to death when One and Two

burst through the door of his chamber, but within a second of drinking a few drops from the phial of water taken from the well of Down Derry he was completely restored to health.

'My wonderful sons!' he said. 'You have risked your lives to find a cure for me. I can never thank you enough. But where is your youngest brother?' he asked, looking around the chamber.

'He got drunk in the inn the day we set out, and he's still sleeping it off,' said Two. 'We tried to wake him, but it was impossible.'

The king was disappointed because, secretly, Three was his favourite son, and he couldn't believe that he would have let him down so badly. He sent his servants to the inn and when they returned with Three the king refused to see him, setting him to work as a servant in the palace kitchens.

And it went on like that for a while, with One and Two basking in their father's gratitude, and Three working his fingers to the bone in the palace kitchens where he slept with the dogs in front of the fire.

Then, one day, two beautiful princesses and their handsome brother rode into the palace keep and asked to meet with the king.

'We would like to see your son,' said the prince. 'We have a gift for him to show our gratitude.'

'I have two sons,' said the king, and he sent for One and Two.

When they were standing before him he asked the prince and princesses which of his sons they were looking for.

'Neither of these two,' said the eldest princess. 'We don't recognise them at all. The boy we are looking for is tall and golden-haired.'

'Well,' said the king, a bit reluctantly. 'There is one other boy, but I've disowned him. I sent my three sons on a quest to find the well of Down Derry and bring some of its healing water to me, but only these two loyal sons of mine returned. The third spent the money I had given him drinking and carousing in the inn down the road.'

'But these two boys of yours haven't been near the well!' said the prince. 'I went to the well with your third son. It was he who brought the water back and he gave some to me so that the enchantment on my sisters and myself could be broken. Not only that, he broke the enchantment that was on the queen in the castle of Down Derry and she's awake and well and running her kingdom again.'

The king was puzzled by this story, which was very different from the one he had been told by One and Two. He sent for Three, who came before him covered in kitchen dirt, his golden hair darkened with grease from the spit.

'That's him!' said the eldest princess, peering at him. For she had been the old woman that had taken him in. 'He spent two nights in my house and I fell in love with him at first sight.'

When the king understood how treacherous One and Two had been he disowned them and sent them into exile, and he restored Three to his position as his best-loved son. Not only that, he made him his heir, which was an honour that had always been set aside for One.

Three married the eldest princess and there was rejoicing throughout the land. When the king died in the fullness of time, Three came to the throne and ruled wisely and well for the rest of his days, even allowing One and Two to return from exile.

The Weasel's Gold

Paddy O'Kelly had had a bad year. His crops had failed and most of his livestock had taken sick and died. All that was left to him were a few scrawny head of cattle and his donkey and he decided he'd have to sell the donkey. He set out early one morning for the fair, driving his donkey before him. It was a fine day to begin with, but then clouds began to gather in the sky and soon it was raining hard. Paddy was too far along the road to go back home, so he decided to keep going. Soon he saw a big house that was set well back from the road. He tied the donkey to a tree beside the house and knocked on the door, hoping to ask for shelter. The door swung open and Paddy walked into the house, calling out for the owner.

It was gloomy in the hallway of the house, but when his eyes had got used to the dim light Paddy saw a door in the corner. When he opened it he was on the threshold of a large room, with a huge fire burning in the hearth. There was no one in the room, so he went up to the fire to warm himself. As he stood there, a huge weasel came through the door, went over to the far corner of the room and dropped something onto a shining pile before running out the door.

As soon as the weasel had disappeared Paddy went over to the corner, where he discovered that the shining pile was a mound of gold sovereigns, enough to fill the large sack that Paddy had brought with him for the things he was going to buy at the market. He scooped up all the coins and put them into the sack, then he went outside, tied the sack onto the donkey's back and set off down the road as fast as he could travel.

He hadn't gone far when he heard the weasel running after him, screeching loudly. She had soon caught up with him and jumped on his back. She was trying to get hold of his throat when two men came along the road with a big dog, who chased the weasel into a hole in the ground and stood guard while Paddy made his escape.

When he got to the fair Paddy sold his donkey for a few shillings, then he bought a fine mare with some of the money he had stolen from the weasel. He bought a good saddle and bridle and rode away on the mare, delighted with his good fortune. He watched out for the weasel all the way home, but the dog was still guarding the hole he had chased her into and Paddy was able to finish his journey safely. When he got home he stabled the mare in his cowshed and went to bed.

The next morning Paddy got up early and went out to the cowshed. He hadn't even reached the door when he was almost knocked over by the weasel, who rushed out of a hole under the stable wall. Paddy's dog chased the weasel and pinned her down while Paddy went into the stable. His horse and his cattle and his calves were all dead, their throats torn out by the weasel.

Paddy ran to where his dog was holding down the weasel, but just as he was about to grab her she broke away and ran off across the fields. Paddy and his dog ran after her and after a while they saw her slinking into a little hut that a fisherman had built beside the lake. Paddy crept up to the door and peeked inside. An old hag was hiding in one of the corners of the room.

'Did you see a weasel come this way?' asked Paddy.

'I did not,' said the hag. 'You'd best keep well away

from me for I have a terrible sickness and you'll catch it if you don't get out of here as fast as you can.'

Suddenly, Paddy's dog was at the hag's throat.

'Get your dog off me! Get him off!' she shouted. 'Get him off me and you'll be rich to the end of your days!'

Paddy pulled the dog away, but kept him close.

'Who are you?' he shouted. 'Are you the weasel who killed my animals?'

'I've been cursed for the last 500 years,' said the hag. 'I was turned into a shapeshifter and I've been roaming the world gathering gold wherever I can so that I can pay to be released from the curse. The shape I was cursed with is that of a weasel and it's natural for me to kill other animals. Now I'm tired of living and it's time for me get some peace, but I can't die

unless someone promises to burn down my house with my body in it. If you would do that for me you can have all the gold I've gathered over the centuries.'

'Where's the gold?' asked Paddy, who wanted to believe her but thought her story probably wasn't true.

'It's under that bush in the corner of the field outside,' said the hag. 'You'll find a chest filled with gold if you dig there tonight. A black dog guards the gold, but he's my son, and you've nothing to fear from him. Take the gold and use some of it to buy the house where you first saw me. Take no notice of me at all – I'll be living in the house but I'll die within a month. You must then put a live coal in the cellar and burn the house down. If you don't tell a living soul about me, and do as I ask, you'll be a rich man for the rest of your days.'

Paddy went home and, that night, when the moon

was high in the sky, he went to the corner of the field with a spade. He hadn't been digging for long when he hit something hard and soon he had uncovered a chest. There was a black dog crouching on top of it, but when he saw Paddy he jumped up and ran away across the fields. Paddy opened the chest and saw, for the second time in as many days, something he had never thought to see in his life – a pile of shining gold coins!

He picked up the chest and carried it back to his house, and although he spent the next few days counting the coins, he could never get to the bottom of the chest. He went to town and bought a suit of fine clothes and some good boots and he went to the owner of the house where he had first seen the weasel.

'I'm interested in buying your house,' he said. 'How much would you ask for it?'

'You can have it for whatever you think it's worth,' said the owner. 'People say it's haunted, and I've been trying to sell it for years.'

So Paddy offered a low price and soon he was moving into the house. He found the old woman in bed in one of the upstairs rooms.

'Pay no attention to me, Paddy,' she said. 'Just do what I asked you to do and I'll leave you in peace for ever.'

Paddy went about his business and came and went from the house every day, and he never heard anything at all from the old woman. After a month had passed he heard the banshee crying outside one night and he knew the old woman had died.

He put the chest of gold and the dog outside, then he took a coal from the fire, put it in the cellar and closed the front door. As he stood outside watching, flames began to leap from the windows and soon the whole house was nothing but a pile of ash.

Paddy bought a fine farm and stocked it with cattle and sheep and soon he was married to the finest young woman in the county. She gave him five healthy children and the family always had the best of everything. No matter how much money Paddy spent, his chest of gold never emptied.

The only strange thing about Paddy, and it was remarked upon throughout the county, was that he would never allow a weasel to be killed on his land.

The Three Godmothers

Annie lived in a cottage near the palace with her mother. She was probably one of the most beautiful girls in all of Ireland, and she was definitely the laziest. She never wanted to do anything around the house – she complained that the steam from the hot washing-up water ruined her complexion, cleaning the kitchen stove broke her nails, and scrubbing the floor made her hands rough and red. As for helping her mother with her spinning and sewing – well, that was a fine recipe for coarse hands, and she avoided it whenever she could.

One day the king's youngest son rode by the cottage, just as Annie was being scolded by her mother for sitting down when she should have been helping her with the spinning.

'How could you speak so harshly to such a lovely creature?' asked the prince.

Annie's mother didn't like to admit that Annie was lazy, as she thought it made her look as if she hadn't brought her up properly.

'Oh, the poor girl,' she smiled at the prince. 'She works far too hard! I've just persuaded her to sit down for a while to catch her breath. She'll have to get back to the spinning soon enough, though – I have an order for three fine linen shirts for the end of the week.'

'Well,' said the prince, 'I've never met a girl who enjoyed spinning before. My mother will be delighted! She refuses to let me marry anyone who can't do something useful. We've had long lines of beautiful princesses at the palace gates, but not one of them can do a hand's turn. Could I take your daughter back to the palace to meet the queen?'

'I'm not sure,' said Annie's mother, a bit flustered at the thought of her daughter going to the palace. But she didn't want to admit that she hadn't been telling the truth about Annie's spinning and weaving, so she agreed that the prince could take her to the palace.

The prince helped Annie climb up onto his horse and she sat in front of him as they rode off towards the palace. She was already falling in love with the prince, who was as handsome as she was beautiful, and she didn't really think about the inconvenient fact that she was supposed to be a master spinner. She was more worried about her nails – she hadn't had a chance to do them that morning and she wanted to look her best when she met the queen.

The palace wasn't very far away, and soon Annie was curtseying to the queen. His mother agreed with the prince that Annie was very beautiful, but when he

told that she could spin and sew as well, the queen, as he had anticipated, was absolutely delighted.

'And can you weave, my dear?' she asked.

Annie, flustered by meeting royalty, was completely speechless. She could only manage to nod, blushing slightly at her lie, which just made her seem even more beautiful to the prince.

'Come with me,' said the queen, and Annie followed her to a large bedroom, in one corner of which there was a huge pile of flax.

'The king needs some new shirts,' said the queen, 'and he insists on the very finest linen. I haven't been able to find anyone who can spin a really fine linen thread. If you start first thing tomorrow morning, you should be finished by sundown.'

The queen left the room, closing the door firmly

behind her. Poor Annie looked at the pile of flax, wondering how on earth she was going to spin it into any kind of thread, let alone fine thread. She decided to go straight to bed, hoping that she might dream up a solution to her problem overnight.

The next morning, the flax was still in the corner and Annie's dreams hadn't given her any ideas. She began to cry, and was soon making so much noise that she didn't hear the door opening and closing softly behind her. She had just blown her nose for the tenth time when she sensed that there was someone else in the room. When she turned around she saw an old woman standing in the middle of the room. She had a spindle in the pocket of her apron and a pair of the most enormous feet Annie had ever seen.

'Who are you?' she whispered.

'Dry your eyes,' said the old woman. 'I'm your Godmother Grandfoot, and I'm the best spinner in the kingdom. Leave this to me. All I ask in return is an invitation to your wedding.'

Annie cheered up at the mention of her wedding and she happily agreed to invite her godmother to it. The old woman stood in the middle of the pile of flax with her spindle and began to spin. By the time the sun was setting all the flax had been spun into neat coils of thread. Annie picked one up and let the thread run through her fingers, amazed at how fine it was.

'I can never thank … ', she said, turning around, but the old woman had disappeared.

When the queen arrived an hour later, she was delighted with the thread.

'I've never seen thread of such fine quality,' she said.

Annie beamed, amazed that she hadn't been found out.

'You can weave all that into cloth tomorrow,' said the queen. 'I'll have a loom brought in first thing in the morning and I'll be expecting a fine bale of cloth by sundown.'

Annie realised that she had bitten off more than she could chew. She had done some spinning and sewing with her mother, but the thread had always been given to a weaver, so she had absolutely no idea how to turn it into cloth. She decided to sleep on it, hoping that a solution would come to her in the night.

The next morning, as the sun began to climb above the horizon, Annie was woken by a loud clattering. She sat up in bed, rubbed her eyes and saw that an enormous loom had been set up in her bedroom.

'I'll never work out how to make cloth on that!' she

said to herself, and she began to cry again. After a while she looked around, and there was another old woman standing behind her. She had the widest hips Annie had ever seen.

'Who are you?' asked Annie.

'I'm your Godmother Broadbeam,' said the old woman, taking a shuttle out of her apron pocket. 'And I'm the best weaver in the kingdom. I'll weave this thread into cloth for you if you promise to invite me to your wedding.'

'Gladly,' said Annie, and she settled down happily to watch the old woman's hands flying up and down the loom. Long before sundown all the thread had been woven into a neat bale of cloth. While Annie examined it the old woman disappeared. An hour later the queen arrived to examine the cloth and was amazed at how soft it was.

'It's almost as fine as the finest silk,' she said. 'Make it into 10 shirts tomorrow and the prince will wear one of them when he marries you.'

Annie had never managed to finish a shirt in her life, and the idea of making 10 was too much for her. She gave up all thought of marrying the prince and went sadly to bed.

The next morning she woke up, washed her face and brushed her hair and prepared herself for the walk back to her mother's house.

'Where are you going?' asked a voice behind her. Annie turned around and there was yet another old woman, who had the biggest, reddest nose Annie had ever seen.

'I'm your Godmother Rubyhooter,' said the old woman. 'I'm the best seamstress in the entire kingdom.

I can make 10 shirts for you out of this beautiful linen, if only you'll invite me to your wedding.'

'Of course I will,' said Annie, and the old woman took a pair of scissors and a pincushion out of her apron pocket and she began to cut out the shirts, her hands moving like greased lightning.

By sundown, there were 10 beautiful shirts hanging in the wardrobe. Annie stood in front of the open wardrobe door to admire them and didn't notice the old woman leaving her bedroom. An hour later the queen came to Annie's bedroom and was so pleased with the 10 shirts that she began planning the wedding that night. Annie was worried that she'd have to spend her life as a princess making shirts, but she decided that she'd deal with that problem once she was married.

After the wedding ceremony Annie and the prince and the king and queen all stood in the receiving line at the entrance to the palace ballroom. The guests were all dressed in the finest silks and satins and the ladies were weighed down with jewels. When they were announced and presented to the royal party they bowed and curtsied and then went to mingle with the other guests. Most of the talk was about how beautiful the new princess was.

'And she must be a hard worker too,' said one guest. 'Otherwise the queen wouldn't have let her marry the prince.'

There was a break in the line of guests and then the footman made another announcement.

'The Widow Grandfoot, godmother to the princess,' he droned, and there was the first of Annie's godmothers.

'Why are your feet so enormous?' asked the queen when the old woman curtsied to her.

'I've spent my life with my feet on the treadle, spinning wool and linen,' said the old woman.

'Annie, you must never spin again!' ordered the queen. 'I'm not having my daughter-in-law going around the palace with monstrous feet!'

Then the footman announced another guest.

'The Widow Broadbeam, godmother to the princess.'

Godmother Broadbeam had to turn sideways to get through the entrance.

'Why on earth are your hips so wide?' asked the queen.

'I've spent my whole life sitting at my loom, weaving wool and linen,' was the reply.

'You must never weave again, Annie,' said the queen, and she made a mental note to order her servants to destroy every loom in the palace.

The very last guest to arrive at the wedding feast was the last of the old women who had helped Annie.

'Your nose is ridiculously red,' said the queen. 'You can't have been born like that.'

'A lifetime of sitting over a pile of sewing has made all the blood run to my nose,' said Godmother Rubyhooter.

The queen was horrified.

'Never pick up a needle again, Annie,' ordered the queen. 'From now on the village seamstress will make all the prince's shirts.'

Annie enjoyed the rest of the marriage banquet, safe in the knowledge that she would be living a long and happy life as a very idle princess.

The Seven Stupid Brothers

Long ago in County Mayo there was a rich farmer
called Seamas Reagan. He owned vast tracts of land
that stretched out farther than the eye could see and
he had herds of cattle and flocks of sheep so large they
couldn't be counted in a day. He had seven fine sons and
everyone said that Seamas Reagan was a lucky man.

But Seamas didn't feel so lucky. He had seven fine sons
all right, but they were growing up faster than the weeds
at the roadside and with as little sense. They showed no
interest in the farm and were just happy to live from day
to day lazing around and eating the meals their mother
cooked for them.

'Those sons of yours are bone idle!' he used to shout at
the poor woman. 'They seem to think money grows on
trees!'

When the youngest son grew into manhood Seamas decided to build each of his sons a house and give them a small piece of land to farm. The seven sons were happy, looking out the windows of their houses at the cattle in their fields.

One day Seamas sent the brothers off to the cattle market at Killala with 21 head of cattle – he didn't think three head of cattle each was too much for his sons to manage.

They hadn't gone far along the road when they met Paddy O'Toole, one of Seamas's neighbours, who was very envious of the fine herd of cattle that the Reagan boys were driving along the road.

'Where are you off to this fine morning?' he asked.

'To the cattle market at Killala fair,' said the eldest Reagan. 'Our father wants us to sell these fine cows.'

'But did you not know that those cows are bewitched!' said Paddy. 'If you sell them you'll bring a world of misfortune down upon yourselves!'

'Father never said anything about that,' said the youngest Reagan. 'What are we to do?'

'Sure, I'll take them off your hands for the price of their skins,' said Paddy. 'The curse never sticks to the skins. I can give you a shilling for each cow, so you'll have a whole guinea between you to spend at the fair.'

That seemed like a good bargain to the seven brothers, so they shook on it, handed over the cattle, pocketed the money and continued their journey to the fair. Paddy, meanwhile, drove the 21 head of fine cattle back along the road they had come to his farm.

When the brothers arrived at the fair everyone crowded around them, amazed that they were there without their father. Delighted to be the centre of attention, the eldest brother bought drinks for everyone, and the guinea they had been given by Paddy O'Toole was soon gone. Empty-handed and with their pockets turned inside out, the brothers headed for home, staggering slightly after the few glasses of whiskey they'd had.

When Seamas saw them coming down the road, giggling and singing, he swore that he'd never let them loose with the cattle again. Life went on in the same way as before, with Seamas doing all the work while his seven sons lazed around. Then, one day, he dropped down dead, followed a week later by his wife.

The eldest brother, Conor, inherited everything that Seamas hadn't already given to the brothers, and he let his riches go to his head. He bought expensive furniture and fine clothes and a herd of pedigree cattle to stock his fields. One day he put on his finest clothes and rode the best horse in his stable into town, where he went into the best tavern, which had a little gilded barrel hanging outside the door.

Whatever he ordered, he gave the landlord three times what he asked for it, and the landlord soon saw that he might do well out of his foolish customer.

'What's that little barrel?' asked Conor.

'That?' said the landlord. 'Why, it's a mare's egg, of course.'

'And will you get a foal out of it?' asked Conor.

'Of course I will,' said the landlord. 'Any day now.'

'I never saw such a thing,' said Conor. 'Would you sell it to me?'

'I will not,' said the landlord. 'It's about to hatch out a foal worth at least 20 pounds.'

'I'll give you 20 guineas for it,' said Conor, 'if I can take it home with me today.'

'Done,' said the landlord, and he took the barrel off its fixings. 'Take care you don't drop it on your way home.'

Conor handed over the 20 guineas, which was all the money he had left in the world, climbed on his horse and cantered home. He was about halfway home, congratulating himself for his cleverness in buying such a rare and valuable thing, when he met his six brothers.

'What have you got there, Conor?' asked Liam.

'It's a mare's egg,' said Conor proudly. 'Did you ever see such a thing?'

He handed it down to his brother, but they each thought another brother was holding it and it hopped out of their grasp and off down the hill with it, rolling faster and faster as it went. It finally came to a stop when it rolled into a big bush on the side of the hill. This startled the hare that was hiding in the bush and it jumped out and went off down the hill as fast as it could travel.

'Look! Look! There's the foal! The egg has laid the foal!' cried Conor, and the seven brothers set off down the hill after it, but the hare had disappeared over the next hill by the time they got to the bottom of the first.

The brothers went home and over the next few months their stupidity made them very poor. Their neighbours decided they were too stupid to be rich and they took advantage of them at every turn. The brothers sold horses and pigs for bits of coloured glass that they believed were jewels and they sold off their houses and land for magic charms that turned out to have no powers at all. One cold day when most of their land and livestock had been sold, Liam was sitting beside the fire. He threw on so much turf he was soon as hot as a spit-roast and when his brother James came in he sent him for the mason to see if he could move the chimney to the other side of the room.

James did as he was asked and soon the mason was knocking at the door.

'If it isn't as hot as hell in here!' he said, when Liam opened the door. 'What can I do for you, Liam?'

'Can you move the chimney to the far side of the room?' asked Liam. 'I get far too hot where it is at the moment.'

'Right so,' said the mason, chuckling to himself.

'It's a messy job, though, so you'd best go off out for a walk while I'm doing it.'

'And what will I owe you for the job?' asked Liam, congratulating himself on being clever enough to ask the price of a job before it was done.

'Well, seeing as it's yourself, I'll only ask for that meadow next to my land.'

'It's a deal,' smiled Liam, and off he went for a walk.

He had no sooner closed the door than the mason picked up Liam's fireside chair and put it against the wall on the far side of the room.

'Now, isn't that better?' he asked Liam when he came back after his walk.

'Much better,' said Liam, sitting down in his chair. 'I was getting far too hot where it was.'

After a while, the brothers were so poor they couldn't afford to buy food, but the wives of the men who had tricked them out of their fortune felt sorry for them and organised a rota to bring them food. And so they went on living in the last house that remained to them, eating food that was given to them. The neighbours, with Paddy O'Toole as the ringleader, were out to get the house from the brothers as well, but as hard as they thought, they couldn't come up with a decent plan.

Then, one warm day at the end of summer, Paddy O'Toole was walking home from town. He saw the seven brothers at the side of the road, sitting in a circle, facing each other as if they were playing some sort of game.

'What are you doing?' asked Paddy.

'Well, Mr O'Toole,' said Brendan Reagan. 'It's like this. We can't get up.'

'And what's to stop you getting up?' laughed Paddy. 'Didn't you get down easy enough?'

'We can't get up because we can't for the life of us tell which feet belong to which of us. If we try to get up we might end up with the wrong feet, and then where would the next man be?'

Paddy had a hard job swallowing his laughter.

'If I tell you how to find your feet, what will you give me for my trouble?' he asked innocently.

'Anything at all, Mr O'Toole, if you can just get us on our feet again!' chorused the brothers.

'Will you give me that house of yours?' asked Paddy.

'We will indeed,' said Conor. 'What good is a house to us if we have to sit here for the rest of our lives not knowing who belongs to which feet?'

Paddy went over to the nearest tree and broke off a good solid branch. He began to beat the brothers around the shoulders and they soon jumped up, shouting out in pain. When they stopped shouting they looked down at their feet in amazement, wondering how they had all managed to find the right ones. They turned to thank Paddy O'Toole, but he was off down the road on his way to take possession of their house.

And from that day on, the brothers wandered the land, begging for food and shelter. But they didn't really mind, because they were too stupid to realise how much they had lost.

The King's Huge Appetite

King Cathal of Munster was a great warrior and a good king, loved throughout his realm. His kingdom was calm and his subjects were happy until a demon came to live inside him. From that day onwards the king was always hungry, and no matter how much he ate, his hunger was never satisfied. He ate all day long, from the moment he woke up in the morning until he lay down again at night, and he was often found raiding the kitchens in the middle of the night.

After four years it looked as if his huge appetite would be the ruin of his kingdom. The king had eaten almost the entire store of food in Munster, and people were beginning to wonder how they would get through the winter.

Meanwhile, in the northern kingdom of Armagh, there lived a clever young scholar who was famous far and wide for his talent for solving difficult problems. When word of King Cathal's huge appetite reached him he thought long and hard about the king's hunger and the problems it was causing for his people.

One fine autumn morning the scholar got up early, packed some of his texts, said goodbye to his family and went off down the road towards Munster, a stout staff in his hand to help him on his way. In return for some storytelling he was offered hospitality here and there all the way through Leinster, and after several long days he arrived in Munster. He knocked on the door of the first big house he came across. The owner of the house was one of King Cathal's most loyal subjects, Pichan. He offered the scholar food and a bed for the night and they stayed up into the small hours, telling stories and making merry. But the next morning Pichan was serious.

'We have a great trouble in our land,' he said to the scholar.

'I had heard of it,' said the scholar.

'The king is coming here tonight with all his court,' said Pichan. 'I have to provide a great feast for all his nobles and their wives, but feeding the king is the greatest trouble to us. He just can't stop eating – my storehouse will be empty by the time he leaves, and I don't know what we will eat this winter.'

'I might be able to help you,' said the scholar. 'I think I know how to solve the problem of the king's huge appetite.'

'If you can do that,' said Pichan, 'I will reward you with my finest flock of sheep.'

The scholar spent the day consulting his texts, and he was waiting with Pichan when the king arrived with his retinue, which snaked behind him as far as the eye could see.

The king had no sooner dismounted his horse when he put both hands into a barrel of apples standing beside the door and had eaten six apples before Pichan could speak a word of welcome.

Meanwhile, the scholar had picked up a stone and was gnawing it with his teeth.

'What on earth are you doing, you mad scholar?' laughed the king. 'You'll break all your teeth doing that!'

'I don't like to see you eating alone,' said the scholar, 'and it looks as if you need all the apples in that barrel.'

The king was ashamed and threw some apples at him, to the amazement of everyone who saw it, because he had not given away a morsel of food for almost four years.

'Give me one more thing,' said the scholar.

'Name it,' said the king. There was something about the scholar that he couldn't quite put his finger on and he wanted to find out what he was up to.

'Fast with me for one night,' said the scholar, 'and I will rid you of your demon.'

And although the demon inside him was gnawing at his belly, the king agreed, and he and the scholar passed a sleepless night together in the great hall of Pichan's house, singing songs and telling stories.

In the morning, the scholar called for a fine breakfast to be brought and soon the table was heaving under platters of bacon, beef, bread and honeycombs. The scholar lit a fire in the great fireplace, and the big oak logs were soon burning with such heat that there was no smoke coming from the fire at all. The scholar put all the meat on huge spit and placed it over the fire.

The king looked as if he was being driven mad by the smell of the roasting meat and the scholar called for ropes to bind him to his chair. Then he placed himself next to the fire, carved the cooked meat from the spits and put each piece on a fork. He dipped it in honey and brought it close to the king's mouth … then he ate it himself!

The king was roaring with anger and hunger. He ordered his servants to kill the scholar, but although the servants had no idea what the scholar was up to, no one obeyed the king.

'I had a dream about you one night,' said the scholar to the king, continuing to eat the meat he cut off the spit, passing it in front of the king first.

'And what did your dream tell you?' asked the king, who was drooling uncontrollably.

'Well,' said the scholar, 'I had heard about your problem, so for one week I burned special herbs each night before I slept. On the seventh night my charm worked and in my dream I met a druid. I asked him what would cure your problem.'

'And what was his solution?' asked the king, convinced that the scholar was completely mad.

'He said we should do exactly what we're doing now,' said the scholar, taunting the king by passing yet another piece of bacon dripping with honey under his nose. As he moved his arm away the demon came roaring through the king's mouth and jumped right into the fire.

Quick as a flash, the scholar covered the demon with an upside-down cauldron and stoked up the fire beneath it until it was blazing fiercely, with huge orange and red flames leaping up the chimney. It wasn't long before the people outside the house saw the demon leaping from the chimney and disappearing into the clouds above.

The demon was never seen again, and the king was so grateful to the scholar that he gave him a room in his palace, a cow from each farm in his realm and a sheep from each field. The scholar sat in the place of honour at the king's right hand at every meal, and the king, cured of his terrible craving for food, became known for the very small size of his appetite.

The Dream of Angus Óg

While Angus, the youngest son of the Dagda, High King of the Sídhe, was sleeping in his chamber one moonlit night he saw a beautiful young woman standing at the end of his bed. She had long black hair and green eyes and wore a golden necklace around her slender neck. Angus stretched out his hand to her, but as soon as he was close to touching her she disappeared. When he woke up the next day there was no sign that she had been in his chamber.

All that day his thoughts were filled with her and he felt, again and again, the disappointment of her disappearance before he could touch her or speak to her. He went to bed early that night, hoping she would come to him again in his dreams.

When he was fast asleep the beautiful young woman appeared again, this time with a harp on which she played the sweetest music Angus had ever heard. As soon as he reached out his hand to touch her, she disappeared, no word having passed her lips.

Every night for a year and day Angus was visited by the young woman, and each night she disappeared without speaking a word. Then the visits stopped as suddenly as they had begun and Angus began to pine away, refusing to eat or take any exercise. Soon he fell ill and no druid in Ireland was able to find a cure for him.

One day a druid came to Angus's home and when he was told that the youngest son of the house was ailing he asked to see him. As soon as he laid eyes on him he could see that the young man was wasting away for love of a woman. Angus told him about the

beautiful young woman and her harp and how she had come to his chamber every night for a year and a day.

The druid spoke to Angus's mother, Boann, and he told her to search the length and breadth of Ireland for the young woman. He told her that Angus could not be saved unless the young woman was brought to him as soon as possible.

So Boann sent messengers to the furthest corners of Ireland, but after a year and a day they had not found the young woman.

'Send for the Dagda,' said the druid, 'so that he can speak to his son.'

But when the Dagda came he could do nothing for his son. He went to see Bodhb, the King of the Sídhe of Munster, who was renowned for his wisdom.

'My son has been wasting away for two years

for love of a young woman who came to him in his dreams, but no one can find her,' he said to Bodhb. 'I'm afraid he will die if she is not found soon.'

He described the young woman to Bodhb, who sent his own messengers on a quest for someone of her appearance. After a year they found someone of her description at Lough Beul Draguin among a company of beautiful women. Bodhb reported their findings to the Dagda, who immediately sent for Angus to see if it was the woman who had appeared to him.

When he was given the news that the young woman had been found Angus jumped off his bed and rode in his chariot for three days and nights until he reached Bodhb's fort.

Bodhb welcomed Angus with a feast, as befitted the son of the Dagda, and after three days they went down to Lough Beul Draguin. As soon as Angus saw the group of young women he was able to pick out the woman of his dreams. She was the only one among them wearing a golden necklace.

'Who is she?' asked Angus.

'She is Caer, daughter of Ethal of the Connacht Sídhe,' replied Bodhb. 'But Ethal will not allow you to take her away.'

'What can I do?' Angus asked the Dagda. 'I will die if I can't have her with me.'

'We will go to see Queen Maeve of Connacht and Alill her husband. She is from their province and they may be able to persuade Ethal to release her to you.'

So the Dagda set off for Connacht, with a great retinue, and was welcomed by Maeve and Alill, who held a great feast that went on for a week, as was the Dagda's due. But when the Dagda asked if they would speak to Ethal on his son's behalf they said they had no power over him to ask him to do anything. However, Alill agreed to send a messenger to Ethal.

When the messenger returned he said that Ethal had refused to come to the court and had said that he would not give his daughter to the son of the Dagda.

Alill and the Dagda were greatly angered by this and they set out with a company of soldiers. Ethal was captured and brought before Alill.

'Give your daughter to the son of the Dagda,' he ordered, although he knew that he was not in a position to command Ethal.

'I cannot,' said Ethal. 'She has been cursed, and can take the shape of a woman only one year in two.'

'And what about the other years?' asked the Dagda.

'She must take the shape of a bird,' said Ethal.

'Which bird?' asked Alill.

'From next month she will take the shape of a swan at Lough Beul Draguin, and her hundreds of handmaidens will also take that shape. If you go there, you will see her, but if Angus wants to be with her he must take her shape each time she changes.'

Ethal was then set free and the Dagda went home and told Angus about everything that had happened.

The next month Angus set out for Lough Beul Draguin and saw two hundred white swans on the water, each with a silver necklace around its neck. He stood right at the edge of the water and called out for Caer.

'Who is calling me?' asked Caer, appearing from the multitude of swans, her gold necklace shimmering in the sunlight.

'It is Angus,' he said. 'I have come to be with you. If the only way I can do that is to take the shape of a swan myself, I am willing to do it.'

So Caer came to the edge of the water and Angus put his two hands on her and he was immediately turned into a swan. They flew up into the air together and travelled to Brú na Bóinne, accompanied by music so sweet that anyone who heard it fell into a deep sleep for three days.

Angus and Caer stayed together for ever, spending one year in human form, and the next in the shape of birds, usually swans.

And to show his gratitude for the part they had played in bringing him to Caer, Angus helped Maeve and Alill when they got involved in the Cattle Raid of Cooley, the Táin Bó Cúailng. But that's another story.

The Black Horse of the Wes

Once upon a time there was a king who had three sons. The king ruled over a very small kingdom and was not rich. When he died his few possessions wer divided between his sons. The eldest son was now the king of the small kingdom and he told his two brothers that he could not support them so they would have to seek their own fortunes. He gave his best stallion to his younger brother, who set off for the eastern kingdoms.

The only thing the youngest son got was an old white pony with a bad limp. There wasn't even a saddle to go with him, just an ancient tattered bridle.

'Oh well,' said the youngest son, whose name was Fiachra, 'we'll just have to make the most of it.'

The old white pony neighed his agreement, and Fiachra put on the bridle and climbed on his back. They set off in a westerly direction but the pony's lame leg meant that they made slow progress. Halfway through the day Fiachra decided to stop so that the pony could have something to eat. He was lying on the grass as the pony munched around him when he thought he noticed something coming out of the western sky. Startled, he stood up. As the object came closer he saw that it was a man on a fine black horse.

Fiachra rubbed his eyes in disbelief, as the horse landed gently on the ground beside him.

'Hello, Prince,' said the rider.

'I'm not much of a prince,' said Fiachra. 'I've had to leave my father's kingdom, and all I have in the world is this poor lame pony.'

'I think your pony would suit me better than this wilful and stubborn horse of mine,' said the stranger. 'Could I persuade you to swap?'

'Well, if you're sure,' said Fiachra, thinking that he would make much better progress on a horse with the full command of his four legs, although he did wonder why anyone would want his lame pony.

'Done,' said the stranger. 'The only good thing about this black horse is that he will take you anywhere you want to go. Apart from that, he has no good qualities – none at all.'

Fiachra got on the fine horse and rode away without a backward glance. As he rode along he began to think about how he had always wanted to see the Kingdom Under the Sea. The horse picked up his pace until they reached the water's edge and then they were going down, down, down under the waves. Soon they came to a large space with a young man sitting on a shell throne in the middle, his long green hair waving gently in the water. He was surrounded by courtiers, all of them with dark green hair and pale green skin.

Fiachra got down off the horse and walked towards the throne.

'Who are you?' he asked the young man who was sitting on it.

'I am the son of the king of this realm,' said the young man. 'Who are you who comes to disturb us?'

'My name is Fiachra, and I'm a prince like yourself,' said Fiachra. 'My black horse brought me here without being asked to do so, but I've always wanted to see this kingdom of yours.'

'Well, Prince,' said the prince of Under the Sea, 'it is no matter to me how you came to be here, but now that you are in front of me, I command you to bring me the princess of the Western Kingdom before sunrise tomorrow.'

'How am I supposed to do that?' thought Fiachra, walking away and mounting the black horse. They rode out of the water and Fiachra got off the horse to think about how he could go about doing what he had been commanded to do.

'I don't even know where the Western Kingdom is!' he exclaimed. 'How on earth can I find the princess and bring her back to Under the Sea?' The horse tossed his head and neighed. 'Don't worry, my prince,' he said. 'I can find the princess of the Western Kingdom.'

And off they galloped, into the west. After more than half a day, the horse slowed down.

'We're almost there,' he said. 'Now, when we get there, we won't go into the town. The princess sits in her window at the top of the castle all day long and she'll see us down below. There are no horses in the town, so she'll want to have a ride on me. Tell her that she must ride in front of you.'

And that was how it turned out. The princess, who was very beautiful, with the longest and shiniest golden hair Fiachra had ever seen, leaned out of her window as soon as she saw him passing by and asked for a ride on the horse. She didn't want to ride in front of Fiachra, but when she tried to mount the horse on her own he reared up on his hind legs and she fell off. This happened three times, so Fiachra climbed into the saddle and lifted the princess up in front of him. Then, almost without their noticing that they had left solid ground, they were up in the sky. When they reached the coast they went right down under the water and soon the princess was standing before the green-haired prince.

'Now that you're here,' said the prince, 'we'll get married without delay.'

'Not so fast,' said the princess. 'If I'd known I was coming here to get married I'd have brought the silver cup my grandmother had for her wedding. I can't marry without it.'

'Well, Prince Fiachra,' said the prince of Under the Sea, 'you'll just have to go back and get the silver cup for the princess.'

Fiachra climbed on the black horse and galloped away. As soon as they were out of earshot he asked the horse if he knew how to get the silver cup.

'I do, actually,' said the horse. 'We'll go straight back to the Western Kingdom where you can mingle with the courtiers who are comforting the king for the loss of his daughter. The silver cup will be handed from one person to another, because it's a ceremonial cup that's used on important occasions. When it comes to you, put it under your arm and leave. I'll be waiting for you outside.'

As soon as they reached the castle Fiachra went inside and it all happened as the horse had said. He arrived back at the Under the Sea just before sunrise and handed the cup to the green-haired prince.

'Excellent,' said the prince, turning to the princess. 'We can be married this evening.'

'But I will need the ring my grandmother and my mother wore on their wedding days,' objected the princess.

'This is getting ridiculous,' said the prince. 'I can't wait for ever.'

'Well, I'm not marrying you without it!' shouted the princess as she stormed off.

The prince commanded Fiachra to get the ring and bring it to him the following day.

'Is the ring in the palace as well?' Fiachra asked the horse as soon as they were out of earshot.

'No,' said the horse, 'this task is a bit more difficult. We have to pass over a mountain of snow, a mountain of ice and a mountain of fire in order to get the ring. But do as I say, and we'll be back here with the ring by tomorrow evening.'

Away they galloped through the cold air.

'Strike me as we come to each mountain,' said the horse, and as they approached the mountain of snow, Fiachra struck the horse with his crop. With one bound the horse was over the mountain, and the same thing happened when they got to the mountain of ice and the mountain of fire. The horse didn't jump quite high enough to clear the flames as they jumped over the last mountain, but they weren't even singed, and when they came through the wall of fire Fiachra could see a town in the valley below.

'Go into the town,' said the exhausted horse, 'and find the blacksmith. Ask him to make 50 short iron spikes.'

When Fiachra came back with the spikes the horse ordered him to stick them into him, far enough that they wouldn't fall out. Fiachra felt bad about doing it, but the horse insisted. Then he said he was going to the lake at the end of the valley.

'As soon as I enter the lake it will go on fire. If the flames go out before sunrise, you may expect to see me again. If they continue to burn, leave this place, for there will be nothing more for you here.'

And so the horse went into the lake and suddenly the whole lake went on fire as if there were a layer of oil on the water. Night fell, and still the lake was burning as if it would burn for ever. But, then, just before sunrise, the flames died away and the black horse rose out of the water with just one spike still stuck in his back, and a silver ring on its end.

The horse came to Fiachra, who took the ring and pulled the last spike out of the horse. Then he mounted the horse and they rode up into the air and reached the Kingdom Under the Sea just as the sun was disappearing into the water.

'Have you brought the ring?' asked the prince impatiently.

'I have,' said Fiachra, 'so you can marry the princess whenever you like.'

'Not until you build me a castle,' said the princess.

'You heard her,' said the prince to Fiachra. 'And before sunrise, if you please!'

Fiachra didn't see how building a castle in a night would be possible, especially as he knew nothing about building.

'This is easy,' said the horse once they were back on land. They were suddenly surrounded by masons and carpenters, all hard at work, and by sunrise the castle was ready.

The princess demanded to inspect it before she would agree to the wedding.

'Well, it all looks very fine,' she said, 'but it lacks one thing.'

'What's that?' asked the prince.

'It needs a well, so that water can be fetched even if the enemy is at the gate.'

So the well was made, and it was so deep it was impossible to see the water at the bottom. The green-haired prince leaned over the side of the well to get a better view and the princess came up behind him and pushed him in.

'If I have to get married,' said the princess, 'I'll marry the man who carried out all the tasks.'

So Fiachra and the princess were married, and the black horse was an honoured guest at their wedding.

Early the next morning Fiachra went to see the horse in his paddock. 'I can never thank you enough for everything you've done for me,' he said to the horse.

'You can thank me by taking your sword and

cutting off my head,' said the horse.

Fiachra stepped back, horrified.

'I can't do that!' he said.

'Do it,' said the horse, 'or I'll do it to you!'

And so, with a heavy heart, Fiachra took his sword and cut off the horse's head.

'Thank you, brother-in-law,' said a voice behind him. When Fiachra turned around he saw a tall handsome stranger, all dressed in the finest black velvet.

'I am the brother of your princess,' said the stranger, 'but I was cursed by a witch so that I could never inherit my birthright. I needed someone to keep me long enough to complete all the trials we've been through together, and you were the only one who could stay the course. My sister knew how I could be released from the curse, which is why she directed you to carry out such impossible tasks. And now you have, and I have been released, and you have my eternal gratitude.'

And the handsome stranger bowed to Fiachra and disappeared into the mist.

Fiachra and the princess lived happily ever after, and every now and then they heard stories about the Black Prince, who had returned to his father's house and was preparing for the day when he would inherit his kingdom.

St Kevin and the King's Goose

It's well known that St Kevin of Glendalough had a way with animals, but not many people know how an animal helped him to found one of the most important monasteries in Ireland.

Kevin was born to a noble family in 498 in the province of Leinster and was sent to a monastery in Cornwall when he was just seven years old. He had a very bad temper and was very grumpy, but he loved animals. There is a story that he came across a bird building a nest on the first day of Lent one year and was so afraid that he would disturb it that he stayed completely still, not moving a muscle, for the whole six weeks of Lent!

When Kevin came back to Ireland as a young man he wanted to set up a monastery at Glendalough, but the King of Glendalough was a pagan and refused to give him permission, no matter how many times he asked. So Kevin just built a little cell for himself there, and lived there on his own, praying that the king would have a change of heart.

One day, when Kevin was walking beside the lake near his cell he met the king. The king was looking very sad and weary and Kevin asked him what was wrong.

'Well,' said the king, 'my poor goose is ill and can hardly fly any more, and I'm afraid she's going to die.'

What really troubled the king was that he believed his own life and health depended on the life and health of his pet goose. When the goose fell ill, he became ill too and he thought that if the goose died so would he.

'I can help your goose,' said Kevin. 'I'll ask God to cure her and she'll be as young and lively as ever she was.'

'Can you really help her?' asked the king, who was prepared to try anything. 'I'll reward you well if you restore my goose to health.'

'I don't want your money,' said Kevin, who had taken a vow of poverty and had turned his back on gold and silver and other riches.

'Well, there must be something you need,' said the king. 'I own everything here for miles around.'

Kevin thought that this might be a good time to ask for some land to build his monastery.

'If I cure your goose, perhaps you could let me have a bit of your land for the monastery,' said Kevin, although he had been refused so many times before.

The King didn't really believe that Kevin had the power of healing, but even so, he wasn't prepared to promise to give him huge tracts of land. 'If you heal my poor goose you can have as much land as she can fly over on her first flight,' he said, thinking that Kevin wouldn't get much more than a small field, and that if the healing worked it would be a price worth paying for his own health.

So the bargain was struck and the king summoned the goose. The poor creature wasn't even able to fly to him, but waddled slowly along the path until she had reached his side. Kevin, who loved all animals, felt his heart go out to the poor creature.

'This goose of yours will be restored to health as soon as you say the word. Are you willing to keep your promise to me?'

'Of course I am,' said the king impatiently, thinking

only of how his own health might be about to improve. 'Get on with it!'

Kevin leaned down and made the sign of the cross on the goose's back, and then whispered something to her. She took off up into the air and flew off to the west as far as the king and Kevin could see, and then she flew off to the north and the east and the south. After what seemed like hours the goose finally returned and landed beside the king.

'I've kept my word,' said Kevin to the king. ' Your goose is as healthy and lively as a gosling again. Now it's up to you to keep your word to me and give me all the land that she flew over.'

The king, who was feeling stronger already, reluctantly agreed that Kevin had lived up to his side of the bargain. Even so, he asked his lawyers if there was any way out of the deal. Eventually, when he realised that he would have to honour his promise, he called his scribes and told them to draw up the documents for the land transfer to Kevin.

The king and his goose lived happy and healthy lives for a few years, and then the goose ate too much dinner one day and died. The king, still convinced that his own health was connected to that of his goose, fell sick and died about two months later.

Kevin was able to build a monastery at Glendalough, helped by the monks who came from far and wide to join him there. When it was built he went to Rome for relics for the altar. It became one of the most important seats of learning in the country. Kevin lived for more than a hundred years, dying in 618, surrounded by the monks and brothers in his beloved monastery. The little cell he built for himself when he

was a young man can still be seen in the remains of the
monastery at Glendalough – it's called St Kevin's Bed.

St Columba and the Battle of Cúil Dreimhne

St Columba, or Colmcille, was born in County Donegal in 521 into the powerful O'Neill clan of Ulster. He was given the name Criomthain, and was later called Columba, which means 'dove'. It is said that he had the gifts of prophecy and healing. He predicted many things that came true and he performed many healing miracles during his lifetime. However, despite the gentleness of his name he was well known for being very hot-tempered and argumentative, and when he was younger he caused a terrible war between two clans. This is how it came about.

When he was still a boy Columba decided that he wanted to be a priest. He was sent to Clonard Abbey in Leinster to study under St Finnian, who had a great reputation as a scholar and teacher. St Finnian had a very beautiful Book of the Psalms, or Psalter, which was his pride and joy. It had been written by hand and beautifully and colourfully decorated by the monks in the scriptorium of the abbey. Columba was very envious of his teacher's beautiful book and nothing would satisfy him but to make a copy of it for himself. But he didn't ask Finnian for his permission to make the copy and when Finnian found out what Columba had done he was very angry. He told Columba that because the original book belonged to him, so did the copy, and he demanded that Columba give it to him. But Columba had put a lot of work into making the copy and he wasn't prepared to give it to Finnian. Even though all the other monks tried to persuade him to give the book to Finnian, Columba dug his heels in and refused to hand it over.

But Columba didn't realise just how angry his teacher was. When he refused to hand over his copy of the Psalter, Finnian went to Diarmuid, the High King of Ireland. He asked him to decide who was in the right in the dispute he was having with Columba. Because Columba was a prince of one of the most powerful clans in Ireland, he probably thought that Diarmuid would say that he was in the right. But Diarmuid considered the matter carefully and finally decided that the book belonged to Finnian.

'To every cow its calf,' he said, 'and to every book its copy.'

Columba thought that this judgment was unfair, and instead of accepting it and giving his copy of the Psalter to Finnian, he decided to go to war. He called out every clan in Ireland that had allegiance to the O'Neill clan and they marched against Dermot.

He met them with his own army and there was a great battle, known as the Battle of Cúil Dreimhne. Although Columba's army was victorious, many people were killed, and it was all because he was too proud to accept the king's judgment and deliver his copy of the Psalter to Finnian.

After the battle Columba's eyes were opened to the dreadful consequences of his pride and he decided his penance would be that he would go into exile, leaving the country of his birth for ever. He set sail for Scotland with 12 monks and they founded a monastery on the island of Iona.

Columba never returned to his beloved Ireland. For the rest of his life he travelled around Scotland, converting the people there to Christianity. Because of this, Columb is as important in Scotland as he is in Ireland. The Scots even have a legend that he tamed the Loch Ness monster

Columba foretold the day of his own death. When the time came he went to the church at Iona and he died at the altar, just as he had foreseen. It was the year 597 and he was 76 years of age, which was very old in those long-ago days. He is the patron saint of County Derry and is one of the Twelve Apostles of Ireland, all of whom studied under Saint Finnian at Clonard Abbey.

St Brigid's Cloak

S t Brigid was born in 450 in Faughart, near Dundalk in County Louth in the province of Leinster. Her father was Dubhthach, a pagan chieftain, and it is thought that her mother was Portuguese, brought to Ireland and sold as a slave.

Brigid was named after the pagan goddess of fire. Her life was hard – she lived the life of a servant instead of that of the daughter of an important chieftain – and it was her father's intention to marry her to someone who would increase his own riches.

However, when she was still just a girl, Brigid heard St Patrick preaching and she decided to convert to Christianity. She made a promise to herself that she would spend her life caring for the poor and the sick. She knew that it would be difficult for her father to

find a husband for her if she was no longer beautiful, so she prayed that her beauty would be taken away from her. But even that didn't persuade her father to let her enter religious life. The final straw was when she began giving away his possessions to the poor people who came to their house. When Brigid gave her father's jewel-studded sword to a beggar, Dubhthach realised that she would never do what he wanted her to and he finally gave her permission to enter a convent. Young women came flocking to join her and Brigid decided to found her own order.

However, she had no land on which to build a monastery and her father refused to give her a plot. She asked the king of Leinster, who was very mean, and never gave anything to her for her charitable work, if he could spare her a bit of land for her monastery. He refused, again and again.

One day she asked the king if she could have just as much land as she could cover with her cloak. He laughed at the idea but told her to go ahead and pick a spot for her monastery.

Brigid put her cloak on the ground and four of her sisters picked up a corner each and ran off in opposite directions. The cloak grew and grew, unfurling itself over the ground as they ran. When it grew too big for four to manage, more sisters ran to take up the edges and soon they had disappeared from view, with the cloak spreading across the rich lands of the Curragh.

'Stop! Stop!' shouted the king. 'If it goes on like this you'll have covered all my lands in Leinster!'

'It serves you right for being so mean,' said Brigid. 'I just wanted a few acres in an out-of-the-way spot so that I could build a monastery.'

'Well,' said the king. 'I suppose you can have a few acres, but please call your cloak back!'

'And you'll be generous to my charities too?' asked Brigid, thinking that she might as well make the most of it.

'Oh, all right so,' grumbled the king. 'Just fold up that ridiculous cloak of yours!'

Brigid built her monastery beside an oak tree that stood on the spot where the town of Kildare was built much later. It was one of Ireland's most famous monasteries and had an art school that taught the skills of metalwork and manuscript illumination.

Whenever Brigid asked the king of Leinster for money for her charitable works, she had only to touch her cloak to make him send his servants running for a bag of gold.

Brigid died in 525. She was 75 years old and had founded many convents all over the country. She is one of the patrons of Ireland and is known as Muire na nGael, which means Our Lady of the Irish. Her feast day is on 1 February, which is considered to be the first day of spring in Ireland. There is a tradition of making St Brigid's crosses on that day, using rushes that have been pulled out of the ground instead of being cut. Brigid invented the cross as a way of explaining the meaning of the Christian cross to people. The crosses are placed over the doors of people's houses, as protection against evil and fire.

Niall of the Nine Hostages

There was a high king of Ireland in the fourth century whose name was Eochaid. He was a wise and powerful ruler and he had a beautiful queen called Mongfind, who gave him four fine sons. They were named Brian, Alill, Fergus and Fiachra. But after a skirmish with the Saxons of Britain, Eochaid had taken several noble hostages back to his palace at Tara, and one of them, Caireann, was so beautiful that the king soon fell in love with her.

Mongfind was terribly jealous of Caireann, and treated her like a slave instead of the royal hostage she was. When she discovered that Caireann was expecting the king's child she made her do all the heavy work in the palace, in the hope that she would lose the baby.

But Caireann was young and strong, and she was also clever, and when her baby boy was born she left him on the grass and went inside, not telling anyone what she had done. She was afraid that if Mongfind knew she had had the baby she would kill him out of spite. When the servants saw the baby lying on the grass they were too afraid of the queen to pick him up.

And so the baby lay there for several hours until a druid called Torna came along. When he saw the baby he picked him up and immediately had a vision. He recognised the child as Eochaid's son and he knew that he would grow up to be a great king whose descendants for generations after him would be kings of Ireland. However, he also knew that the boy was in great danger if he stayed at Tara.

So Torna took the baby away and raised him in secret. He gave him the name that had come to him n his vision, Niall, and gave him an even better education than the king's four older sons were getting at Tara. When Niall was of age, Torna brought him to Tara to lay his claim to the throne.

As soon as they were through the palace gates Niall saw his mother, Caireann, drawing water from the well. She was dressed in rags, but when Torna whispered to Niall that she was his mother, the young man recognised her for who she was and told her to drop her buckets. He brought her into the palace and dressed her in robes of royal purple.

When Mongfind saw Caireann in all her finery she was furious, but Eochaid recognised that Niall was his long-lost son and he was delighted to see him at Tara. Mongfind realised that her own sons' position at court was in danger and she demanded that Eochaid name his successor to his throne – in those days the king's eldest son wasn't automatically his heir; it was up to the king to decide who would take the throne when he died.

Mongfind was sure that Eochaid would choose his eldest son, Brian, or one of her other sons, but Eochaid did no such thing. He said that the decision was not his to make, but that he would give each of his five sons a test – whichever of the young men did best in the test would succeed him. He asked his druid to devise a suitable test of kingship.

This was a difficult thing, even for a druid, but eventually he told the five sons of Eochaid to go to the forge where they should each make a weapon for themselves. He told them that they would be judged by the type and craftsmanship of the weapons. But as soon as they had all entered the forge, the druid closed the door and set the forge on fire. The heir to the throne would be the person who saved the most valuable thing from the forge.

Brian was the first to emerge from the forge, his eyes streaming from the smoke. He was carrying the great hammers and the druid said that this meant he would be a strong fighter. Fiachra came next, carrying a cask of water, which meant he would be an artist and a scientist. Alill brought a chest filled with weapons, and the druid said that this showed he would defend the people. Fergus, always the weakest son, came out with a bundle of kindling, and the druid said that this meant that he would never have children. Then Niall emerged from the smoke, carrying the heavy anvil on which all the weapons at Tara were made, and the druid told Eochaid that this meant that Niall was the anvil on which the power of the people of Ireland would be forged, and that he should be the next high king of Ireland.

Eochaid, who was delighted with his new-found son, was more than happy to accept the druid's judgment, but when he told Mongfind she was furious. She insisted that all five of the king's sons fight it out to see who was the strongest, and she secretly told her sons to gang up on the newcomer. But Torna, realising that Niall was in grave danger, told the king that Niall should be his successor, and Eochaid agreed.

It seemed then that the matter was settled, but Mongfind refused to give up hope that one of her sons would be high king one day. She refused to allow Eochaid to announce that he had named Niall as his heir, hoping that he would change his mind and that Brian or one of her other sons would reign one day.

One day, all five sons went out hunting. They caught a deer and made a fire to cook it, but it was only after they had eaten that the realised they hadn't brought any water with them. They sent Fergus to see if he could find some water for them, but there was no stream nearby. He was on his way back to his brothers when he found a well, hidden in some bushes, but it was guarded by the most fearsome hag he had ever laid eyes on. She had just one eye, long filthy nails and coarse, greasy hair. Her teeth, when she smiled at him, were green and crooked, and she was dressed in the filthiest rags imaginable. However, although he was curling up with disgust inside, Fergus was well brought up and he asked her politely if he could have some water for his brothers.

'Yes,' said the hag, 'but you'll have to give me a kiss first.'

'I'd rather die of thirst,' said Fergus, forgetting his manners, and he ran back to his brothers and told them that he couldn't find a well anywhere.

One by one each of Mongfind's sons tried to persuade the hag to let them have a drink without kissing her, but to no avail. They each came back and said that there was no water to be found. They all sat around the fire, getting thirstier and thirstier, until Niall said that he would try to get something to drink for them.

It didn't take him long to find the well and he was amazed that his brothers had missed it. When he saw the hag he asked if he could have some water.

'Yes,' said the hag, as she had said to his four brothers, 'but you'll have to give me a kiss first.'

'Gladly,' said Niall, and he approached the hag and kissed her. And as his lips touched hers she was transformed into a beautiful young woman, with golden hair and teeth like pearls. She told Niall that he was going to be one of Ireland's most famous kings, and that his descendants for generations to come would also rule the country.

'Take some water back to your brothers,' she said, 'but before you let them drink, be sure to make them swear allegiance to you. When you get back to Tara tonight, declare that you are the king's heir as soon as you go through the gates of the palace.'

So Niall brought the water back to his four brothers and they swore allegiance to him. Then they drank and drank and drank until they were no longer thirsty. To be honest, they didn't mind if Niall became king – they liked him and they were happy enough enjoying the easy life of royal princes without the responsibility of ruling the kingdom.

The brothers went back to Tara and when they hung up their weapons in the great hall, Niall hung his above theirs. This was a sign, recognised by everybody at Tara, that he was the first among them. When they sat down at the table, Niall sat at the head, opposite the king. When Eochaid asked his sons how the day's hunting had gone, Niall answered for all of them.

'Why are you speaking for my sons, who are older than you?' thundered Mongfind. 'You are in no position to speak for them!'

But Brian told her that all four brothers had sworn allegiance to Niall, and that he would succeed their father when the time came.

When Eochaid died, Niall was crowned king of all Ireland. He ruled wisely and was known as a peacemaker rather than a warmonger. At that time kings used to take hostages in order to keep the peace. The hostages were usually royal or noble and were treated well. Kings were unlikely to attack if their sons or daughters were being held hostage. Niall took hostages from the five provinces of Ireland and from the kingdoms of Scotland, England, Wales and France, which is how he came to be known as Niall of the Nine Hostages.

Luath and the Red Champion

L uath was a poor fisherman who lived a simple life in his small hut near the beach. He longed for something exciting to happen to him, but every day was the same as the day before and he knew that the next day would be the same as today.

Every morning after breakfast Luath went down to the seashore to mend his nets, ready for the evening's fishing.

One day, as he sat on a rock mending the holes in his nets, he saw a small currach coming towards him over the waves. As it approached the shore he saw that there was just one person in it – a tall young man with red hair who was hitting a silver ball from stern to prow of the currach with a dazzling golden hurl.

When the currach was almost on the beach, the young man jumped out and pulled it up onto the shingle.

'Good day to you, sir,' said Luath. 'What brings you here?'

'I had a yearning to go somewhere I'd never been before,' said the young man, 'and this seems like a pleasant place.'

'It is,' said Luath, 'although nothing exciting ever happens here.'

'Why don't we play a game of dice together?' said the young man. 'Best of three throws? You never know, life just might get a bit more exciting for you.' He drew two dice from inside his tunic and sat down beside Luath.

'What will we play for?' he asked.

'If I lose you can have everything I own,' said Luath, thinking that he owned so little he wouldn't miss it. 'And if I win, I'd like to have the field beside my hut filled with fine cattle.'

The young man agreed to the stakes and he threw the dice. Luath won all three throws.

'Will you play another game?' asked the young man. 'We could make it the best of three games?'

'No,' said Luath, who knew that you should stop while you were ahead, 'one is enough for me.' The young man pushed his currach into the sea and soon he had disappeared over the horizon. Luath made his way home and he was no more than halfway down the road when he saw that the field beside his little hut was full of fine black cattle.

The next morning Luath went down to the beach again and the young man with the red hair was already there, sitting on the rock. He asked Luath if he would play another game of dice for another stake.

'If I lose,' said Luath, confidently, for he didn't think that the young man was very good at dice, 'you can have everything I own. And if I win, I'd like the other field beside my hut to be filled with sheep.'

So they played another game, and Luath won again, and again he refused to play a second game. The young man climbed into his currach and disappeared over the horizon while Luath made his way home. When he got to the top of the road he could see that the field on the other side of his hut was filled with fluffy white sheep.

That night Luath could hardly sleep for excitement. As soon as the sun had risen he was down on the beach, but even though he was much earlier than usual the young man was there before him, sitting on the rock in the sunshine, throwing his dice from one hand to the other.

'So,' said the young man, 'what are the stakes today?'

'If I lose, you can have everything I own,' said Luath, 'but if I win I want a fine castle and a beautiful wife.'

The young man agreed and they played a game. Again, Luath won, and again he refused to play a second game. He was so eager to get home that he didn't even wait to see the young man get into his currach. When he reached the top of the dunes he could see a fine castle in the distance, colourful pennants flying from its turrets. He hurried along the road and was greeted at the drawbridge by the most beautiful woman he had ever seen.

'I am your wife,' she said, 'and glad to be, now that I've met you, although I have no idea at all how this has come to pass.'

Luath told her about the games of dice he had played with the young man, but she said nothing.

The days rolled into weeks and the weeks rolled into months and Luath was enjoying his new life. Then he began to think that he needed some gold and silver and jewels to go with the fine castle and the beautiful wife. One morning he told his wife that he was going down to the beach to see if he could find the young man.

'Whatever you do, don't play another game of dice with him!' she called after him as he went off down the road, but her words were blown away by the wind.

When Luath arrived on the beach the young man

was already there and Luath wondered if he had come every morning since he won his castle and his wife.

'Will we play for the usual stakes?' asked the young man, who didn't seem at all surprised to see Luath.

'Yes, we will, everything I own, as usual, and this time I'd like a room full of silver and gold and fine jewels,' said Luath, looking forward to his life as a very rich man.

The young man threw the dice and won. Luath threw them and lost. The same thing happened three times. Luath had lost! He didn't believe it.

'Can we make it the best of three games?' he asked.

'No,' said the young man. 'You wouldn't do it before, so you can't do it now.' And without a backward glance he climbed into the currach and sailed away.

Filled with fear, Luath set off back to his castle, but by the time he was halfway down the road he could see that it was gone. There were no fields filled with fine black cows and fluffy white sheep, just his shabby little fisherman's hut. When he got to the door there was no beautiful wife waiting for him.

And it's said that every morning for the rest of his life Luath went down to the beach hoping to find the young man sitting on the rock, but he never laid eyes on him again.

Fionn Mac Cumhaill and the Building of the Burren

Long ago, in the days of Fionn Mac Cumhaill and his brave warriors, the Fianna, all the land in County Clare was fresh and green with stones dotted around the fields. There was no sign of the strange flat limestone landscape that we know today as the Burren. This is the story of how the Burren came to be.

King Aengus of Clare was well known for his huge feasts and generous hospitality. No one who came to his door was ever sent away hungry. However, the fame of his annual eel feast on 1 May spread so far and wide that he had to hold a lottery every year instead of inviting guests in the traditional way. On this particular year, Fionn Mac Cumhaill and the

Fianna had won invitations and they had been looking forward to the famous eel feast for months.

The best place by far to get eels was Doolin and cartloads of them were sent to Aengus's palace for the feast every year. In the last week of April all the king's servants were preparing for the great feast when a messenger rushed into the palace, breathless and dishevelled. He was brought before the king.

'The fort at Ballykinvarga has been invaded and the villains won't allow any eels from Doolin to be brought across their land unless you give them a sack of gold,' he panted.

'No eels at the feast of eels?' asked the king. 'We can't have this. It's just as well Fionn and the Fianna won invitations to this year's feast. Fetch them here and we'll sort this out.'

Fionn had arrived at Aengus's palace with 20 of the Fianna the day before. They were all enjoying the break, looking forward to the feast and a few days off with no work or fighting. Then the king's messenger arrived.

When the king told Fionn that he needed the help of the Fianna they set off immediately, thinking that they'd be able to sort everything out very quickly and they'd be back with the eels long before the feast.

'The feast is in just three days,' the king reminded them. 'If we don't have the eels by then it'll be a disaster.'

Fionn and the Fianna marched off towards Ballykinvarga, but as soon as they got there they realised they'd walked into a trap. The invaders of the fort were standing on the ridge above them, preparing to roll down huge boulders on top of the marching men.

'Shields!' shouted Fionn at the last moment, and the Fianna raised their shields to make a roof over their heads so the boulders bounced off them. The boulders were followed by a shower of arrows, which glanced off the shields and fell harmlessly to the ground.

'Draw swords!' shouted Fionn, and the Fianna drew their swords and charged up the hill. But by the time they got to the top, their ambushers had retreated inside the fort and bolted the heavy doors against them.

The Fianna proceeded towards the fort, but they looked around them carefully as they went, expecting to be ambushed again at any moment. They made camp below the walls of the fort, but they passed a cold night because they were afraid a fire would give their position away.

The next morning, Fionn explained his tactics to the Fianna.

'I know Ballykinvarga well. The fort has only one entrance and they'll have it well defended. There's more of them than us and we'd never beat them if it came to a fight. So we have to be clever about it and use whatever tactics we can. If they won't let us pass and refuse to promise safe passage for the eels we'll insult them and hurl abuse at them. That'll get them really riled, and when they've fired all their weapons at us, we'll take the fort and kill them all.'

Fionn sent three of the Fianna, including his right-hand man, Conán, up to the gate of the fort to give the men inside a message. When they got there they asked the gatekeeper if they could have a word with their leader. A few moments later an ugly face peered over the wall of the fort.

'Well,' said Conán, recognising the face, 'if it isn't One-Eye, you ugly brute! I knew I should have killed you the last time we met. Now, are you going to give us free passage, or do we have to come in there and kill the lot of you!'

The response was a shower of arrows, but they all fell wide of their mark, and Conán and his companions were back with the rest of the Fianna in no time. They started hurling abuse at the men in the fort, shouting that their mothers were lazy and their fathers were greedy, that their cats were mangy and their dogs were cowardly curs, that their horses were bony nags that wouldn't get as far as the next fort. The abuse got worse and worse every time they opened their mouths. When their opponents ran out of arrows they started throwing down rocks and the Fianna threw them back, and when they ran out of rocks to throw they tore up the boulders from the surrounding countryside, digging right down into the ground to liberate the huge slabs.

Soon the Fianna had thrown so many rocks and boulders the fort was beginning to disappear. After a few hours it had been buried completely, with the men still inside.

'Do you think they're dead?' asked one of the Fianna.

'It doesn't matter,' said Fionn. 'As long as they're trapped there they can't make a nuisance of themselves.'

Their enemy dealt with, the Fianna went to Doolin as fast as they could.

'We've less than a day to get the eels back to the king,' said Fionn, when they arrived in Doolin and found the eels waiting for them in barrels, ready to go.

But the horses that were supposed to pull the carts had been stolen the night before, and nobody was able to think of anywhere that might have replacements. There was nothing for it but for the Fianna to pull the carts themselves. Fionn organised them so that there were two men to a cart. They set off at a quick pace and people lined the roadside along the way as if they were running a race.

However, even the Fianna couldn't run as fast as horses and it was dark on the evening of the third day when they finally rattled up to the palace. The king had been waiting on the battlements for hours, and he was in a frenzy.

'I hear no horses yet!' he kept shouting. 'Where are my eels? Where are my eels?'

The servants were getting more and more nervous – Aengus was well know for his fiery temper.

'Look, your majesty!' said one of the servants, finally, tugging at this sleeve. 'Here they come!'

Well, the king laughed and laughed when he saw the Fianna pulling the heavy carts into the courtyard. They were so exhausted they had no words with which to respond, which was probably just as well, because they thought he was being very ungrateful.

They went off for a well-earned rest while the palace cooks started preparing the eels for the feast. They cooked them every way they could be cooked – fried, roasted, boiled, made into pies and casseroles. The food was brought out to the banqueting hall and soon the tables were groaning and sagging under the weight of the platters. The feast lasted for a day and a night and it was a great success. Everyone said it was the finest eel feast ever. The Fianna slept through it, and didn't wake up for a full three days. When they finally roused themselves, all the eels had been eaten, every last one. All they could do was dream about next year's feast – they considered that they were entitled to another invitation, lottery or no lottery. They promised themselves that they wouldn't arrive until the doors of the banqueting hall were being opened to admit the guests to the feast.

The next day, just as Fionn and the Fianna were preparing to go home, they heard ructions from outside the gate of the palace. There was banging on the gate and shouting and general hullabaloo. Eventually the king went up to the battlements and looked over the wall at the crowd gathered outside his palace.

'What's wrong with you?' he asked. 'What's all the noise about?'

'We've come from the Burren,' the people gathered below shouted angrily. 'Our land is all torn up by the

Fianna. They trampled all over it and destroyed all our boundary walls. It's no good to us the way it is. We can't plant anything, we can't graze our animals – it's completely useless!'

'I heard nothing about that,' said Aengus, and he called Fionn to him.

Fionn explained what had happened, and how they'd had to use every rock in the place to bury the fort of Ballykinvarga.

'Well,' said Aengus, 'you'd better get back there and fix it. If you don't I'll have a war on my hands, and I can't afford that at the moment.'

So Fionn and the Fianna went back to the Burren. They weren't too pleased about it and they just picked up the rocks and slabs they had used to bury the fort and threw them down the hillside. They left them where they landed in the fields all around and then they went straight home before Aengus could ask them to do anything else.

The land was still useless to the people, even after they'd tried to tidy it up themselves. Most of the boulders were just too big for them to move, even if they tried to lift them together. They decided to go to Aengus again. When they got to the palace they started shouting and banging and waving their pikes and shovels and shouting about how badly they'd been treated – and complaining that they hadn't even been invited to the eel feast that was the cause of all their problems.

But this time, Aengus didn't listen to them.

'I sent the Fianna to put back the stones they'd lifted from your land and you're still not satisfied. There's no pleasing you. Get off my land and don't show your faces here again.'

And the people went back to their land, but there really was no way they could farm it. Even the strongest of them weren't strong enough to move the stones the Fianna had thrown. In the end the farmers had to move away from that part of Clare, and nothing ever grew there again except tiny little plants that grow nowhere else in Ireland and were able to make their homes in the cracks between the huge slabs of limestone.

Fionn Mac Cumhaill and the Deer

One day, when Fionn was still a very young man, he went out hunting with the Fianna, accompanied by his faithful young wolfhounds, Bran and Sceolán. They had been hunting all day without any success when, late in the afternoon, they spotted a young deer at the edge of the forest.

Fionn and the Fianna chased after her, Bran and Sceolán leading the way, but she was faster than any deer they had ever come across and soon she was far away and out of sight. But Bran and Sceolán had kept up with her, and Fionn soon heard his dogs give the bark that was their signal that they had landed their prey.

Imagine his surprise when he followed the sound of the dogs and found the deer resting on a mossy bank, with Bran and Sceolán guarding her, their heads resting on her flank. Their behaviour was so unusual that Fionn knew that there must be something very special about the deer. He decided to take her home with him and look after her. When he arrived at the palace he gave orders that she was to be kept safe within its walls.

That night Fionn didn't sleep well. He kept thinking about the deer and why Bran and Sceolán had protected her. When he finally fell into a light sleep he was woken by a feeling that the air around him was moving. He opened his eyes and saw a beautiful russet-haired woman walking towards his bed. Her long white gown caught the moonlight coming through the window, and the air itself seemed to shimmer.

'Who are you?' asked Fionn.

'I am Sadhbh,' said the woman, 'and today you rescued me from an enchantment. The Dark Druid turned me into a deer because I refused to be his handmaiden. You have made me safe by bringing me to your palace. The Dark Druid can't reach me as long as I stay within its walls.'

Fionn soon fell in love with Sadhbh, who was not only beautiful, but kind and gentle too, and before long they were married. She refused to go outside the palace walls, because even though Fionn was powerful, he was no match for the Dark Druid's dreadful powers. Fionn and Sadhbh stayed inside the palace for a whole year and Fionn was so happy that he didn't miss the outside world.

Then, one day, a messenger came to the palace with a report that Ireland was being invaded. Fionn had no

choice but to go with the Fianna to fight the invaders and save his country. He didn't want to leave Sadhbh, especially because she was expecting a baby, but she told him to go.

'I'll be safe here, Fionn,' she said as she kissed him goodbye. 'The servants will look after me and I'll stay within the palace walls. I'll watch for you from the battlements every day.'

Fionn and the Fianna galloped away to the coast and there was a fierce battle with the invaders. After a week they had finally fought them back and the survivors limped away to their boats, their tails between their legs.

Fionn hurried home with his men, thinking about how happy he would be to see Sadhbh again. But when he arrived at the palace he didn't see his wife looking out for him, as she had promised. When the palace gate opened and the warriors went inside, Fionn realised that there was an unearthly quiet about the place. Where was all the normal hustle and bustle of palace life? Where, more importantly, was his wife? He began to get a bad feeling in the pit of his stomach.

The servants seemed too frightened to say anything, but finally Fionn's old steward stepped forward.

'Every day your wife walked the battlements, watching and waiting for your return. Some of the servants were always with her. Then, on the fourth day, the servants were surprised to see you coming towards the palace gates with Bran and Sceolán. Sadhbh asked for the gates to be opened to let you in. We thought it was strange that you were alone, without the Fianna, but we thought you'd probably ridden on ahead in your haste to get home.'

The old man faltered, then went on.

'Sadhbh went out to greet you, but the man who looked like you took a hazel wand from inside his tunic and touched her with it. She turned back into the deer she had been when you brought her here, and she followed the man, the two dogs nipping at her heels. The servants armed themselves as quickly as they could, but by then the man and the deer had disappeared.'

Fionn fell into a rage and as soon as the Fianna had rested they went out with him to scour the countryside for Sadhbh. But although he searched for her for seven long years, he never caught sight of the beautiful deer who had become his wife.

One day, after he had given up his search, he went out hunting alone with Bran and Sceolán. They ran off and disappeared, and when he finally caught up with them in a grassy clearing in the forest, they were playing with a young boy, about seven years of age. The boy refused to speak, but Fionn could tell from the way the dogs behaved with him that he must be the son he and Sadhbh had been expecting when he went away to battle all those years ago.

He brought him home to his palace and named him Oisín, which means 'little faun'. Bran and Sceolán went everywhere with him and, after a few months, he began to speak. He told Fionn about his mother, a kind and gentle deer, and about the man who brought food but who was often cruel. One day, the man touched his mother with a hazel wand and she began to follow him. When the man looked back and saw her faun he touched him with the wand, and he turned into the boy Fionn found in the clearing in the forest.

Fionn never saw Sadhbh again, but he raised Oisín well, and when he reached manhood he joined the Fianna and became a proud and fearless warrior who had almost as many adventures as Fionn.

Fionn Mac Cumhaill and the Big Men

One fine spring day Fionn and his men were on the Hill of Howth, admiring the view spread out beneath them. As they gazed at the deep blue sea, its shining surface dotted occasionally by the white horses of gently breaking waves, they noticed a large vessel on the horizon.

The boat came closer and closer to land and it finally came into the harbour. Two sailors jumped out and moored the boat to the dock, then a third man jumped out and joined them. The three sailors straightened their tunics and began to walk towards the Hill of Howth.

As they walked, one of the men picked up a handful of pebbles. He stretched out his arm, with the stones in the middle of his palm. He stroked the pebbles with the fingers of his other hand

'Turn yourselves into a dwelling house,' he commanded loudly. And, to the amazement of the men watching from the hill, a beautiful stone house appeared right beside him. However, it wouldn't have been much good to live in, because the roof had no covering.

Another man picked up a piece of slate from the ground. He held it out in front of him.

'Cover the roof with slabs of slate,' he ordered. And, in an instant, the house had a beautiful, sturdy roof.

The third man picked up a bit of wood and ordered

it to line the walls and ceiling of the house. The words were no sooner out of his mouth than the house was clad inside with beautiful pine boards.

'I wonder who these strangers are,' said Fionn to the Fianna. 'They are not normal men.'

He decided that the only way to find out who they were was to ask them, so he went down the hill to meet them.

'Good day to you,' he greeted them. 'We have been watching you from the hilltop and we are wondering who you are and where you have come from?'

'We have been sent by the ruler of the Kingdom of the Big Men,' said the man who appeared to be the leader of the threesome. 'He has heard of the great Fionn Mac Cumhaill and has asked if he will do combat for him against a monster who has been terrorising our kingdom.'

'Do you know where we can find Fionn?' asked the second man.

'I do not,' said Fionn. 'He went off on a hunting trip with his men yesterday, and we're not expecting him back for at least two weeks.'

'That's a shame,' said the third man. 'But we'll wait here until he returns.'

Fionn also had magical powers but didn't often use them as casting a spell used up all his energy, leaving him exhausted for hours. However, he decided that on this occasion it was something he needed to do, and he put the men under a spell so that they couldn't move from that spot until he released them.

Fionn sat on the grass for a few hours until he felt

his strength returning and then he went down to the harbour and got his boat ready for a journey across the water to the land of the Big Men.

That night, together with his faithful wolfhound Bran, Fionn set sail across the water, with the full moon to guide him and a gentle breeze catching his sail so that he made quick progress across the sea. At dawn he reached the shores of the Kingdom of the Big Men. He pulled his boat onto the beach, well above the tide line, and he set off along the road, walking briskly inland.

About an hour later he met one of the people who lived in the kingdom. He was as big as a giant and he looked curiously at Fionn, who was at eye level with his ankle.

'You'd make a great mascot for the king,' said the

giant. 'He's been looking for a new one for a while. He'd like the lapdog too,' he added. Bran growled at him.

The man reached down, scooped up Fionn and Bran and put them in his pocket, then he turned and walked back up the road to the palace. He told the sentries why he had come, opening his pocket so that they could see Fionn inside it. He was admitted to the throne room, where the king and queen were sitting on their thrones, surrounded by the royal children and all the nobles of the land.

When the king saw Fionn he was delighted, as the man had predicted. He put the tiny warrior on the palm of one hand, placed Bran on the other and paraded through the streets, delighting the crowds of people who had heard about the tiny man and his lapdog.

Back at the palace, the king made up a little bed for

Fionn at the end of his own bed, with a breadbasket beside it for Bran. They all went to bed after a great feast that the king held in their honour and soon everyone was snoring loudly.

Later that night the king rose from his bed at midnight, left his chamber and didn't come back until dawn was breaking, looking absolutely exhausted. The same thing happened the next night, and the next night, and the next night.

After a week, Fionn asked the king why he went out every night.

'I have to do combat with a monster who wants to marry my daughter and take half my kingdom as her dowry.'

'Can you not send your champion to do combat with him?' asked Fionn.

'No one in my kingdom will fight him,' said the king sadly. 'I sent my men over the water to find the great Fionn Mac Cumhaill, for I have heard tales of his strength and courage and would make him my champion, but I haven't laid eyes on my three messengers since the day they left my kingdom.'

'Well,' said Fionn, 'why don't you get a good night's sleep tonight and I'll fight the monster.'

'You?' laughed the king. 'He'd gobble you up in a flash!'

'I have a trick or two up my sleeve,' insisted Fionn. 'Let me go in your place. If I think I can't defeat him, I'll come straight back here.'

'All right, so,' said the king reluctantly, for he had grown fond of his tiny mascot.

That night, as the clock struck midnight, Fionn and

Bran crept out of the palace to the cliff where the king said the combat took place every night. When they arrived there all was deserted, but soon the sea beneath began glowing and roiling and then a huge serpent darted from the water and looked down at Fionn.

'What do we have here?' he roared. 'Such a little man has been sent to do combat with me? What an insult!'

'No,' said Fionn. 'I'm not here to fight you. What chance would I have against a monster like you? I have a message from the king. The queen died today and he asks if you will give him a day to grieve.'

'I will,' said the monster. 'I could do with a night off myself.' And he slid back into the sea.

At dawn Fionn went back to the palace and lay down in his little bed.

When the king woke up he shouted out, 'My kingdom is lost, my mascot is killed!'

'Don't fret yourself, your Majesty,' said Fionn. 'I fought the monster and he has gone away until tonight.'

That night, Fionn persuaded the king to let him go out to the monster again.

'You again?' said the monster when he saw Fionn standing on the cliff.

'I've been sent to tell you that the king has died of grief,' Fionn said, 'and his nobles have asked me if you will give them time to have him buried.'

'Well, all right then,' said the monster, a bit reluctantly, 'but tomorrow night I'm fighting for the hand of the princess in marriage.' And the beast disappeared into the ocean again.

At dawn, Fionn went back to the palace. Again, when the king woke up he was filled with fear and shouted out, 'My kingdom is lost, my mascot is killed!'

'Calm yourself, your Majesty,' said Fionn. 'I fought the monster again. Tonight I will kill him.'

That night, Fionn went down the clifftop with Bran and waited for the monster. 'I'll need your help with this, Bran,' said Fionn. 'Be prepared to launch one of the three poisoned darts you keep hidden in your mouth.'

When the monster appeared out of the sea he asked which champion had been sent to fight him.

'I will fight you,' said Fionn. 'There is no other champion.'

The monster opened his huge mouth and began to roar with laughter at the idea of this tiny man taking

him on in a mortal combat. He was still laughing when Bran launched one of the three poisoned darts from his mouth. It went down the monster's huge throat and the poison shrivelled his heart and lungs. Within a couple of seconds he had fallen down dead.

Fionn took his sword, cut off the monster's head and brought it back to the palace. The king couldn't believe that Fionn had managed to kill the monster. He was delighted that the princess and the kingdom were now safe, but he said that the monster's family would want their revenge.

That night Fionn and Bran went to the top of the cliff as they had done on the previous three nights.

'Be prepared, Bran,' said Fionn. 'The king said last night's monster was the smallest member of his family. We might have a harder job to do tonight.'

Soon enough the ocean started glowing and moving and a monster, much bigger than the one Fionn had killed the previous day, appeared out of the water.

'You murdered my son!' roared the monster. 'You will pay for it with your life!'

The monster's mouth was wide open so that he could roar as loudly as possible. Fionn ran towards the monster with his sword and Bran launched the second poisoned dart from his mouth. It went straight down the monster's throat, making his heart and lungs shrivel up. He fell down dead on the clifftop. Fionn took his sword and cut off the monster's head and dragged it back to the palace.

The king could hardly believe his eyes when he saw the size of the head Fionn had presented him with.

'The monster we really have to worry about is the last remaining one,' said the king. 'You have killed her son and her husband, and she will be out for your blood.'

'Not to worry,' said Fionn. 'If I managed to kill the other two, I can kill this one.'

He was waiting on the clifftop with Bran that night when an enormous she-monster rose up out of the water.

'You killed my son and my husband!' she roared at Fionn.

'I did,' said Fionn. 'And I'll kill you too!' And with that, he stuck his lance in the monster's side. She screamed and lunged at Fionn, trying to tear him with her sharp claws. Bran launched the last of his poisoned darts and it went straight down her throat. Her lungs and heart shrivelled and she dropped down dead. Fionn cut off her enormous head and dragged it back to the palace.

When he saw the head the king ordered three days of feasting and celebration and Fionn had the place of honour at the royal table.

'Who are you?' asked the king. 'It was once foretold that the great warrior Fionn Mac Cumhaill was the only person who could save my kingdom. I sent for him some weeks ago, yet you have come out of nowhere and done what I believed only he could do.'

'I am Fionn Mac Cumhaill,' said Fionn. 'And I have been wondering why you sent for me. Now that the prophecy has been fulfilled I'll be on my way back to my own country.'

The king was sorry to see his mascot leave, but he gave him many valuable things from his own treasury.

'I've managed well enough without the three men I sent to find you,' said the king. 'They are all brave men and they can join the Fianna if you like.'

Fionn went back to the shore and made his boat ready to sail, and then he left the Kingdom of the Big Men with Bran.

When he arrived back at Howth Harbour Fionn removed the enchantment from the three men sent by the king of the Big Men. They couldn't remember why they had come to Ireland, so Fionn invited them to join the Fianna. They took an oath to serve him faithfully alongside his other warriors, and the next time the Fianna were sent for to sort out a quarrel, they were glad that their ranks had swelled, for the three men were strong, fierce and brave and were always happy to use a bit of enchantment to make sure the battle went their way.

Danny Mulready's Dream

Once upon a time there was a man called Danny Mulready who lived in Kerry and worked as a manager on the estate of the big house. Danny had never been greedy or grasping and he lived a quiet and contented life, working hard every day and hankering after nothing.

Danny and his wife Nuala had a nice little house on the edge of the estate with a little patch of land attached to it. While Danny was at work every day Nuala looked after their patch of land. Her vegetable plot was the envy of the neighbourhood. She and Danny had fresh vegetables every day and she preserved enough of them every year to give them a taste of summer all through the cold months. They had no children but were happy enough with their own company.

There was just one thing Danny wanted, and as the years passed it became his heart's desire. Danny wanted to have a dream, for he had never ever had one. He heard people talking about their dreams all the time and it seemed to him that a dream must be a wonderful thing, something that could lift you out of your ordinary life, even if it was only for a few hours. He didn't care if it was a good dream or a bad dream or a frightening dream – he wanted to have just one dream and then, he thought, he could die happy.

One day when Danny was mending the fences that kept the cattle from running all over the front lawn, his master passed by on his horse and they fell into conversation. Danny had been thinking about dreams again and he told his master about his wish to have one.

'Well,' said his master, 'you'll have a dream tonight if you follow my instructions exactly.'

'I'd do anything if it meant I'd have a dream,' said Danny eagerly.

So his master told him how he could be sure of having a dream.

'When you go home tonight, spend the evening as you usually do. Have a meal, tell stories beside the fire and then, when you are ready to go to bed, rake the embers from the hearth and put them out. Instead of going to bed as usual, make up your bed in the empty hearth and sleep there all night. If you do that, you'll have enough dreaming to last you a lifetime.'

That seemed simple enough, and that night Danny raked the embers out of the hearth. Nuala thought he had lost his mind, so he told her what his master had advised him to do.

'Well, then,' she said. 'If that's how it is we'll both sleep in the hearth together.'

They had just fallen asleep when there was a knock on the door of the house. Danny opened the door and found one of his master's servants standing on the doorstep.

'Get up,' said the servant, 'and take this letter from the master to America.'

Danny got dressed, took the letter and set off towards the coast. It was a long way away, and when he had travelled just half the distance, he met a cowherd with his cattle.

'God bless you, Danny Mulready,' said the boy, much to Danny's surprise, for he had never laid eyes on him in his life.

'Where are you going at this late hour?' asked the

boy. 'Most people are tucked up in bed at this time.'

'I'm taking a letter to America from my master – am I on the right road?' asked Danny.

'Yes, you are,' said the boy. 'Just keep going west until you reach the water. But how will you get to America?'

'I'll think about that when I have to,' replied Danny, and off he went again, walking briskly until he reached the coast. There was no boat in sight, but Danny spotted a crane standing on one foot on the sand.

'God bless you, Danny Mulready,' said the crane.

'How is it that everyone seems to know me and I know no one?' said Danny, more to himself than to the crane.

'What are you doing here?' asked the crane, curiously.

Danny told her where he was going, and then he said that he didn't know how he'd get over the water.

'Sit on my back, rest your feet on my wings and I'll take you to the other side,' offered the crane.

'But what will I do if you get tired before we get to America?' asked Danny. 'I've heard it's a very long way and I can't swim!'

'Don't worry,' said the crane. 'I won't get tired before we've arrived in America.'

So Danny climbed on the crane's back, and she rose up over the sea and flew towards the west. When they were about halfway to America she began to slow down.

'Danny Mulready,' she said, 'get down off me; I'm too tired to go another flap further.'

'I can't get off now, over the middle of the ocean,' said Danny, looking down at the endless blue water below with no patch of land in sight. 'You promised me you'd take me all the way there. If you make me get off I'll drown!'

'I don't care,' replied the crane. 'I need to take a rest.' And she began to sway this way and that, trying to shift Danny from her back. If she could have flown upside down she would have, just to get rid of her load.

Danny was clinging to the crane's long neck for dear life, wondering how long more he could hang on for, when he looked down again and what should he see but a boat, a long way off.

'If you'll carry me until we're flying over that boat,' he said to the crane, 'I'll jump down onto it and ask the sailors to take me to America.'

'All right, so,' said the crane, and on she flew until the boat was almost underneath them.

'Throw down one of your shoes, Danny Mulready,' shouted the captain. 'If it lands on deck, jump down after it and we'll take you to America.'

Danny shook his foot until one of his shoes fell off, and it fell down, down, down …

'What on earth is going on!' shouted Nuala. 'What are you doing, Danny!' She looked all around the bed, but Danny was nowhere to be seen.

'What are you doing in that boat, Nuala?' said Danny, his voice coming from the chimney. 'Are you coming to America with me?'

Nuala lit the candle she'd left beside the bed and when she looked up, there was Danny, halfway up the chimney, covered from head to toe with black soot. He had one shoe on and one shoe off, and it was the shoe that had hit Nuala and woken her up.

Danny climbed down the chimney and had a long bath to get rid of all the soot. And nobody ever heard him wishing to have a dream again.